The Great Storm

The
Lone ★ *Star*
Journals

Book 2

The Great Storm

The Hurricane Diary
of J. T. King

Galveston, Texas, 1900

Lisa Waller Rogers

Texas Tech University Press

This book was set in Galliard, and Cosmic Two. The paper used in this book meets the minimum requirements of ANSI/NISO Z39.48-1992 (R1997). ∞

Although his diary is based on historical events, J. T. King is a fictional character.

Series design by Joan Osth; cover art by Mary Ann Jacob

Library of Congress Cataloging-in-Publication Data
Rogers, Lisa Waller, 1955–
    The great storm : the hurricane diary of J. T. King, Galveston, Texas, 1900 / Lisa Waller Rogers.
        p.   cm. — (Lone star journals ; 2)
Summary: A teenage boy keeps a diary of events during the devastating hurricane which struck Galveston, Texas, in 1900, and of the rescue operations that followed.
    ISBN 0-89672-478-6 (cloth : alk. paper)
    1.HurricanesTexas—Galveston—Juvenile fiction. [1.Hurricanes —Texas —Galveston—Fiction. 2. Survival—Fiction. 3. Disaster relief—Fiction. 4. Interpersonal relations—Fiction. 5. Galveston (Tex.)—History—20th century—Fiction. 6. Diaries—Fiction.] I. Title.

    PZ7.R63625 Gr 2002
    [Fic]—dc21
    00-011879   2002000236

01 02 03 04 05 06 07 08 09 / 9 8 7 6 5 4 3 2 1

Texas Tech University Press
Box 41037
Lubbock, Texas 79409-1037 USA

800-832-4042
ttup@ttu.edu
www.ttup.ttu.edu

With love
to the Three Ls of Corpus Christi:
Loise,
Laura,
and
Leigh,
who weathered three fierce Gulf hurricanes:
Carla (1961),
Beulah (1967),
and
Celia (1970).
And to my parents, who weathered them all.

The storm got worse and worse and the water came in under the doors and soon rose higher. We had closed all the doors upstairs that led into the hall, and sat on the stairs as high as possible . . . We soon heard the blinds and windows break in the rooms upstairs . . . It sounded as if the rooms were filled with a thousand little devils, shrieking and whistling.

Louisa Hansen Rollfing
Survivor, Galveston storm of 1900,
from her 1932 memoir

The Great Storm

The Hurricane Diary
of J. T. King

Galveston, Texas, 1900

J. T.'s World

At Momsie's Boardinghouse

J. T.—a teenage boy always on the go, whether it be biking, skating, swimming, waging a peach pit war, or sneaking past a nurse

Momsie—J. T.'s grandmother, who makes great lemon meringue pie

Samson—the "Mr. Fix-it" man at Momsie's

Mr. Plummer—a regular roomer at Momsie's, who likes peace, quiet, and sardines with French mustard

Mrs. Newton—one of the summer people rooming at Momsie's, who has her hands full with twin six-year-olds and a baby girl

University of Texas medical students—Momsie's roomers from September to May, who run on coffee and lightbulbs

Fargo—a little brown dachshund, who is a slave to his nose

Bessie—a faithful mule

At Larchmont Hall

Daisy—a rich teenage girl who reads books in
the treetops

Mrs. Larchmont—Daisy's social-climbing
mother, whose days are a steady round of
calling cards, dinner parties, costume
balls, and meetings at ladies' clubs

Mr. Larchmont—Daisy's very wealthy and very
busy father

Moses—Samson's super-tall brother and Mrs.
Larchmont's favorite footman

Flossie—Daisy's tattletale French maid

Around the City

Ippy—J. T.'s best friend

Willie, Al, and Frank—J. T.'s buddies, who live at St. Mary's Orphan Asylum

Crab Jack—a salty old sea captain

Lucky—Crab Jack's loyal parrot

Madame Matisse—Mrs. Larchmont's French dressmaker

St. Mary's Orphan Asylum

Galveston, Texas

⭐

1900

Sunday, April 8, 1900

I saw it first. My buddies were too busy horsing around to notice.

It was a hot afternoon. Everybody (but I) was taking a cool dip. Some of the guys had stayed close to shore. They were wrestling and smearing gooey sand in each other's hair. Others, though, were way out in the bay. They were swimming behind an old-timey paddle wheeler, taking a wash.

I was the only dry one in the bunch. You see, today is Sunday. My grandmother, Momsie, absolutely forbids me to swim on the Sabbath day. I was stranded on Pier 16, doomed to sit on the sidelines and watch the fun. I slumped against a wood piling, dangling my toes in the cool, green water that licked up at them from below.

It cheered me a bit when I saw Ippy leave the water and walk up the pier toward me.

"Hey, J. T.," he said, chucking me on the chin as he passed by. He stopped at the edge of the pier and leaned into a dive. "Watch this," he shouted back at me over his shoulder. With a graceful, high arc, he plunged into the bay.

Boy, how I wanted to race him. His arms cut through the choppy harbor. He was swimming to the channel marker. Often he and I have a contest to see who can touch the marker first. It's hardly ever a real contest, though. Ippy always wins. He's a natural-born athlete. I'm certainly not. Momsie says that not everyone can be an athlete. She says I have other qualities. She says God gave me a power far greater than athletic power.

"Instinct," she says to me, proudly. "God gave you instinct." She's probably just trying to pump me up.

And then again, maybe not. Because, at that moment, something made me turn away from Ippy and look to his left. It was then that I saw it. A gray dorsal fin was slicing through the water at top speed. It, too, was headed straight for the channel marker.

It was a shark! I jumped to my feet. I felt so helpless, watching from the dock, as the shark's moon-shaped tail whipped from side to side, pushing it closer and closer to Ippy.

"Shark!" I yelled, cupping my hands around my mouth. "Shark!"

But Ippy could not hear me. A lazy Colombian banana boat had just chugged into Galveston Bay. The captain had blown his whistle, drowning out my warning.

Later

It seemed like forever from the time I pulled Ippy from the water till I got him to the hospital. Had that kind man not offered his wagon, Ippy surely would have died. He's lost so much blood from that bite on his foot. The nurse said it's still too early to tell whether he'll keep his foot or not. The doctor was to examine him later.

It was not until Ippy's parents arrived that I remembered Momsie. She must have been worried sick. I'm always on time to help her serve Sunday supper at our boardinghouse, the busiest meal of the week. Not just our lodgers but neighbors, too, show up on Sunday nights, expecting to be fed. I had been so caught up in saving Ippy that I had completely forgotten my duty. I had left Momsie and our handyman, Samson, to handle the big meal alone.

I decided against calling the house, preferring instead to ride straight home and tell Momsie face-to-face about the shark attack. Afterward, then, I could head back to the hospital to hear what the doctor had to say about Ippy's foot.

Usually, if I push it, I can make it across the island on my bicycle in fifteen minutes flat. Sealy Hospital is on the north side near Galveston Bay, where the shark attacked Ippy. Ships dock there to load Texas cotton. I live on the opposite side, just two blocks from the Gulf of Mexico. Summer people flock to our south beach for a seaside holiday.

I plotted the speediest route possible: south on Ninth Street, right on Broadway, left on Twenty-fifth Street. I was eager to get home and set things straight with Momsie.

I jumped on my bike. At first, I made good time. I covered the eight blocks on Ninth Street without a hitch.

It was when I turned right on Broadway that my troubles began. A jolly street party was going on. The trolley car that runs down the middle of the boulevard was hung with colored lights. A brass band was playing. The rich people who live on Broadway were streaming out of their palm-shaded mansions into the streets. They were singing, laughing, dancing—and blocking my path. I couldn't get through the crowd. I had to get off of my bike and walk a zigzag course a whole sixteen blocks. I was really steamed. I lost a lot of time.

I turned left on Twenty-fifth Street, entering the home stretch. I could see the waves breaking on the beach ahead. The sea breeze felt good blowing through my hair and drying my wet clothes.

By the time I reached our house on the corner of Q½ and Twenty-fifth Streets, the porch lights were on. Our two-story house sits high on a hill and looks out to sea. It welcomed me like a lighthouse. I took a sharp right turn into the alley behind our house, skidding and almost crashing into the shed. I leapt off my bike, rolled it behind the fig tree, and made a beeline for the back door.

Dinner was definitely over. Our handyman, Samson, was washing dishes at the sink. I waved and slipped into my bedroom for a quick change of clothes before finding Momsie.

In all honesty, my bedroom isn't a true bedroom. It's a pantry. I share my space with sacks of potatoes and coffee beans, barrels of sugar and flour, drums of lard, and cans of peaches. I sleep on a folding cot. Before my grandfather, Popeye, died last year, I had a real bedroom upstairs with windows opening onto the sea. So did Momsie. Now she sleeps in a little room under the stairs. Momsie had to make a living after Popeye passed away. So she converted our house into a boardinghouse and took in roomers.

"If we are to make ends meet," Momsie reminds me when I miss my old bedroom, "we must give over every available space to the needs and comforts of our guests." She always puts a brave face on everything.

Once I was in my room, I unbuttoned my shirt and tried to pull it off. Ouch! The dried blood made the cloth stick to my skin. I was still peeling the shirt from my chest when I heard a knock at the door.

"J. T., may I come in?" It was Momsie. Would she be mad to discover I had gone swimming on the Sabbath?

"Just a minute," I called, tossing my shirt into the corner and throwing on a robe.

In bustled Momsie, carrying a dinner tray. Nipping close on her heels was our fat dachshund, Fargo. She placed the tray on a fruit crate that doubles as my desk. Ham, potato salad, cornbread, and cold lemonade. Yummmm. I had forgotten how hungry I was. But the food had to wait. First, I had to set things right with Momsie.

I sat down on the cot, patting a spot for her to join me. She plopped down beside me. The fabric of the cot stretched and groaned with her weight. (There's a lot of Momsie.) "Oh, Momsie," I began, "I have so much to tell you. I'm sorry I wasn't here to help you with dinner. You see, something terrible has happened!" Fargo jumped up on my leg, tail wagging. I lifted him onto my lap.

"Now, honey, you can just relax," she said, patting my knee reassuringly. "I know everything. Joe Gilbert called from the hospital just a little while ago and filled me in. He says Ippy's going to be fine. The doctors can save his foot. What I want to know is: are you all right?"

I let out a great sigh. Ippy could keep his foot. "Oh, that's great!" I said. "Oh, and, yes, Momsie, I'm just fine." I turned to face her. "What do you mean, you know everything? Do you know about my swimming on the Sabbath?" I asked.

She nodded.

"And you're not mad at me?"

"Mad at you?" she said. "Mad at you for saving your friend's life?" She reached over and took both of my hands in hers. "Honey," she said, "Let me ask you a question. If Fargo fell into a well on a Sunday, would you go in and rescue him?"

"Of course I would," I said, without hesitating.

"Well, then, isn't Ippy's life even more precious to you than your dog's?"

"Oh, Momsie," I said, springing up and hugging her. "How could I ever have doubted you?" I untied the sash of my robe and began looking for a clean shirt to wear to the hospital.

Momsie fixed me with a stern look. "And just where do you think you're going, young man?" she asked, placing strong hands on my shoulders and forcing me to sit down. "The hospital is closed for the night. The best thing for you to do is to get some food and rest and head over there first thing in the morning. Remember: tomorrow is still a school day."

She was right, as usual. I could go to the hospital first thing in the morning. I gave her a peck on the cheek and Fargo a pat on the head. After wishing them both good night, I closed the door behind them.

I devoured my supper, then collapsed, stuffed, on my cot. I didn't really feel like writing in my diary tonight, but I made myself, as I do every night. Writing about something when it's fresh seals it as a memory forever.

I feel I can drift off to sleep now. I can hear the whistle of a faraway train as it rolls into the station.

Monday, April 9, 1900

Samson was so loud this morning. I know it's rude of me to complain. After all, he was cooking our breakfast. But, gee, what a lot of racket. I mean, with Samson around, who needs an alarm clock? Today, he rattled around the kitchen, lighting the gas in the oven—POOF!—and then slamming the oven door—BANG! Even with a pillow covering my ears, I heard the bacon sizzle and the coffee perk. Up above, the floorboards creaked as the roomers dragged themselves out of bed. Samson had waked them, too. The dread Monday morning was upon us. GROAN! Another school day.

I was just about to doze off again when I remembered. I smacked my forehead with the palm of my hand. Holy moly! What had I been thinking last night? I sat up straight in bed. I had been so tired and preoccupied, I had completely forgotten to make all the lunches. Plus, I was going to try to get to the hospital before school.

It's a good thing Samson had been noisy or I'd have been in a heap of trouble.

I spotted an old pair of pants hanging by suspenders on a hook nearby and threw them on. I'd bother about a shirt and shoes later. I popped into the bathroom and splashed cold water on my face. When I came out, a long line of roomers waiting to use our one bathroom stretched all the way down the front hall and up the curving stairwell. They were the medical students. This morning, our Doctors of Tomorrow were nothing but a bunch of sleepy-eyed guys with firecracker hair, clutching towels, soap, and razors. Not one of them grumbled about having to wait for a shave, though. Most of them come from the country. They are used to getting up with the chickens and sharing one bathroom.

I skedaddled off to the kitchen and got down to business, filling lunch pails. For the medical students and myself, I threw together fig sandwiches, link sausages, hard-boiled eggs, and bottles of root beer. Those guys will eat anything I pack.

Mr. Plummer, though, is a far pickier customer. I have to make him a custom lunch. I always start by including a jug of Momsie's special sugar mint tea, sweaty-cold from the icebox. Today, I rummaged through the pantry looking for special foods to please his fancy taste buds. I found a tin of sardines packed in oil, a bottle of French mustard, some soda crackers, and a jar of marmalade, imported from England.

His lunch costs us a fortune. Once I griped about the extra expense to Momsie.

"Horace Plummer is our number one roomer," she scolded. "He's been living with us since Popeye died.

He's the only roomer who lives here year-round. We depend upon his business." Mr. Plummer lives in my old bedroom. He's the only nonstudent living here.

I thought about Mr. Plummer as I packed his lunch. He works at a downtown printing company on Avenue B, which we call "the Strand." His office is on the second floor of the building. On the first floor is Ritter's Café. How exotic to have a restaurant downstairs. Yet Mr. Plummer does not eat lunch there. I used to wonder why not. I finally asked him about it one evening last summer.

We were eating lemon meringue pie on the front porch swing and watching the waves break on the beach. It was a mild evening. Folks were strolling down the beach and riding in their buggies. I was having my second helping of pie, and Mr. Plummer was having his third.

"Excuse me, sir," I asked him, "but have you ever eaten at Ritter's?"

"Why, yes, J. T., I have," he said. "It's curious you should ask."

"Well, I was just kind of wondering," I explained. "I haven't eaten in very many restaurants. Is the food bad there or something?"

Mr. Plummer paused. "I can't recall whether the food there is good or bad," he replied. "I only know that I can't get any peace down there. The fellows who eat there are always pushing me to drink a glass of beer. I don't like beer. I like Mrs. King's sugar mint tea."

Just thinking about Momsie's sugar mint tea made him want some. He stopped the swing and reached for his glass. After he took a long, wet sip, we resumed swinging. He finished his story. "The way those men at Ritter's carry on, you'd think I was the only man in Galveston who doesn't drink."

A few weeks later, I found out where Mr. Plummer takes his quieter lunch. Ippy told me. Ippy was down on the bay front doing his job, delivering a telegram for Western Union. It was about noon. As he bicycled along, he spotted Mr. Plummer's black bowler hat and handlebar mustache. Mr. Plummer was all by himself, leaning against a big wooden barrel, nibbling on some cheese and tossing breadcrumbs to the seagulls hovering above him.

So I guess I really can't begrudge Mr. Plummer his small pleasures. I finished packing his lunch and stuffed cloth napkins, forks, knives, and spoons in all the lunch pails. Just as I carried the pails to the back porch, the milk wagon clip-clopped into our alley. I hurried down the steps to greet Mr. Harris, our milkman.

As I was picking up the milk jugs, I heard Momsie cry, "Have a good day!" I turned around to look. She was standing on the back porch, pinning the screen door open with her ample frame. The students were leaving for the university—and in a hurry, too. They charged through the doorway like racehorses from the starting gate. They kissed Momsie on the cheek and grabbed their lunch pails. Hugging their books to their chests, they bounded down the steps and ran to catch the streetcar. Those who had not finished breakfast clenched their biscuits in their teeth. Momsie waved. I opened my mouth to cry out good-bye, but nothing came out. I was hoarse from yelling "shark!" so much yesterday.

Once they'd all gone, I thought: Now it's my turn. I grabbed the milk jugs and scurried inside for some of Samson's great bacon and eggs before I opened my diary to record the morning's events.

Look at the time! I have to hurry to make the upstairs beds, if I'm going to see Ippy before school.

Whew! That was a close call with the lunches.

That night

There wasn't time to go to the hospital this morning after all. Luckily though, I got to go this afternoon with my good buddies, Willie, Al, and Frank, who were also at the beach yesterday when the shark attacked Ippy. Just as I arrived home, they drove up the alley in a rickety old wagon. Pulling it was an even more rickety old mule.

Willie, Al, and Frank are orphans. They live at St. Mary's Orphan Asylum a few miles down the beach. Their mother superior, Sister Camillus, let them take the mule wagon to visit Ippy at the hospital and they wanted me to go with them.

Luckily, I had no homework this afternoon. Momsie said I could go over to the hospital once I'd swept the front walk. While my buddies waited, Momsie served them pie in the parlor.

I like to play with the orphans, but they play a lot rougher than my other friends. Willie is always punching my arm until it's black-and-blue. And then there's Al—when we go swimming, he dunks me five, six, sometimes seven times in a row. I swallow so much salt water that one day I'll sink like a lead weight and drown. Frank, though, is not so rowdy. He's quieter and smaller. He came here from Poland with his parents, who died from yellow fever. So many children in the home were orphaned by disease. Maybe Frank will talk more when he learns to speak English. Willie is teaching him.

I put up with their rough-and-tumble games because they're much more fun to be with than the guys from school. For one thing, they don't complain much. They're grateful for even the smallest kindness—like being served hot apple pie on Momsie's best china. They hate being motherless and fatherless. It's really sad.

Come to think of it, I guess I'm a sort of orphan, too. My mother died giving me birth during the hurricane of 1886 (I will turn fourteen this coming August 20). Papa died two years ago in the Spanish-American War. A Spanish soldier shot him as he charged up San Juan Hill with Theodore Roosevelt. My papa is an honest-to-goodness American hero. His sword hangs over our fireplace.

I finished my sweeping, and the boys put their dishes in the sink. The four of us hopped in the wagon. Fargo went, too. Willie took the reins. Even though Willie clicked his tongue and shouted, "Giddy-up!" that old mule seemed to take his own sweet time getting us to

Sealy Hospital. We were so anxious to see Ippy, and had to be home in an hour.

Oops. Momsie just hollered, "Lights out." It's later than I thought. I'll write more about Ippy tomorrow night—

Tuesday, April 10, 1900

Well, we almost didn't get to see Ippy yesterday afternoon. It was nearly 5:00 by the time we reached the hospital. We tried to slip past the third-floor nurse's station, but the nurse stopped us.

"And just where do you think you're going?" she asked, coming out from behind the desk. She put her hands on her hips.

We told her we'd come to see Ippy.

"Oh, no, you don't," she said. With outstretched arms, she blocked the swinging doors to Ippy's ward. "What's the matter, can't you boys read?" she asked, pointing to a sign on the wall beneath a clock. The sign said, "Patient Visiting Hours: 7:00–8:30 P.M."

"Come back at 7:00," she barked, storming back to her desk.

But we couldn't come back at 7:00. If we wanted to see Ippy, we decided, it was now or never. Our buddy needed us.

We pretended to leave by ducking into a stairwell. As we waited for the coast to clear, I noticed a janitor's cart abandoned at the other end of the hall. It was piled high with scummy mops, dusty brooms, wadded-up towels and sheets, and other truly disgusting but gloriously tall stuff. It gave me a great idea.

Here was the plan. We made Willie the "janitor." From a supply closet, we found him a jacket and a cap. His job was to stand at the back of the cart and push. Our job was to hide. Al, Frank, and I crouched down alongside the cart, squeezing between it and the wall. Our team's mission was to make it to Ippy's room before that janitor came looking for his cart.

While Willie strolled along at a fast clip, we three hunchbacks had a terrible time keeping up with him and staying hidden. I was nervous. We got nearer and nearer the nurse's station. I heard her pen scratching the paper. Sweat collected behind my knees, trickled down my calves, and bounced off my socks. With four wheels and eight legs, we kept moving. My comb kept falling out of my pocket, so I ended up clenching it between my teeth. That made me drool. I think I swallowed a hair. I pictured myself as a snail. The cart was my shell, and I was oozing a slimy trail of sweat and drool . . .

Then I heard someone shout, "Hey!" The janitor! I thought. My neck tensed up. Any minute, I expected some muscle-bound fellow to reach down and collar me. But nothing happened. We sailed past the nurse's station and landed in front of Ippy's ward.

We were almost inside when Al messed up. As he straightened up to walk, his shooter marble fell out of his pocket. We watched in frozen fear as the big marble hit the floor, bounced a couple of times, and began its slow roll across the clean floor. We knew that when it hit the other wall, it would go PING! Then, sure as shooting, that nurse would look up from her paper-work and catch us.

But miracle of miracles, when that marble hit the wall, it didn't go PING! It went BONG! BONG! BONG! BONG! BONG—or, rather, the clock on the wall went BONG! It was 5:00. We slipped through the swinging doors undetected.

Ippy was lying in a bed beneath a window. His skin looked like white turkey meat gone three days bad. He was a grayish, greenish color. He'd lost a lot of blood.

It was a shock to see such a sturdy boy in such a sorry state.

We were so glad to see him, but we didn't have a lot of time for niceties. We got right down to business. "Tell us what happened," we demanded, all at the same time.

Ippy was drowsy. That's some strong medicine they're giving him. When he talks, he slurs his words—which are hard enough to follow normally, because he speaks half-English and half-Italian, and sometimes even his English is a mystery. Of course, he always throws in a lot of arched eyebrows and arm gestures, which help you catch the overall drift of what he is saying.

Here, I think, is what Ippy told us about the shark attack: "It's still mostly a blur. I don't remember much. I just know that I was swimming along when something began tugging at my left foot. I remember thinking that my foot was caught in a steel trap. What are traps doing out in the bay? I thought. And then it dawned on me. A shark had ahold of my foot.

"That shark shook my foot like Fargo shakes a rat. He shook and shook and shook my foot. He was trying to rip it off my leg. I had to think quickly. I pulled back my free leg and kicked him—BAM!—in the snout. It worked! He let go of my foot. As he swam off, I saw the cold gray gleam of his killer eye. It gave me the willies.

"I didn't know then how much of my foot was left—I just felt a gigantic jab of pain. I was swirling in a pool of blood. I felt dizzy and sick. The last thing I remember is a strong arm around my neck and someone dragging me to shore."

At that point Ippy's eyes grew wide, and he looked at me. "Was that you, J. T.?" he asked.

I nodded.

He extended his hand. "Thanks, buddy," he said, and we gave each other the club handshake. I'd gone in the water and saved him, saved him from drowning— Ippy, the champion swimmer. It felt good.

His doctors say that his foot will be fine. Sure, it's swollen and scraped and has a few puncture wounds. They say he needs to stay off it for two weeks. And I say it'll never happen. If I know Ippy, he'll be back on his bicycle before the week is out. He can't miss work. His family needs the money.

Ippy's full name is Carlo Ippolito. He and his family came here from Italy a few years back. They all found work in a textile factory. The factory was hot, dirty, and dark. The work was hard, and the days were long. The pay was pitiful, but it put bread in their mouths. But

26

then, unexpectedly, the factory closed. Ippy's whole family was out of work.

The Ippolitos were starving. Then one day, Ippy found a check for five hundred dollars. He walked into the Western Union office and turned it over to the manager. The manager was so impressed with Ippy's honesty that on the spot he gave him a job delivering messages. The rest of his family now works for Crab Jack, an old sea captain who runs a shrimping business.

Wednesday, April 11, 1900

At breakfast this morning, I told Samson about Ippy. Samson was glad to hear that Ippy would make it, but he fixed me with one of his stern looks.

"What's wrong, Samson?" I asked.

"It's just that you can't go around spreading this here shark story," he said. "It'll only upset people. Next month the students will be leaving to go back home for vacation. That'll leave three empty rooms upstairs. Hopefully, tourists will come from Houston, San Antonio, and Dallas and rent those rooms for the summer. Do you think those summer people are gonna come to our island if they think sharks are gonna eat up their babies?"

He has a point. If we are going to make a living, I have to keep my mouth shut. Nevertheless, there is danger in the water—terrible danger. I don't know which is scarier—knowing about that danger or not knowing—

Sunday, April 29, 1900

Yesterday was the greatest day. Ippy and I found a rowboat. We were catching crabs on the East Beach when we stumbled upon an old boat washed up on shore. It had a hole bashed in its side. It had probably broken loose of its moorings somewhere up the coast, drifted south, and crashed into the jetty rocks.

We couldn't believe our luck. Imagine—having our very own boat. Oh, the places we could go . . .

"If we can get it fixed," said Ippy, "we can row over to Pelican Island and have an oyster roast." We knew exactly who could fix it, too: the old sea captain, Crab Jack. He is wise about anything involving boats or the sea. We decided to pay Crab Jack a visit.

With a big heave-ho, I emptied out our bucket of blue crabs, sending a tangle of claws, shells, and curved legs scrambling back into the sea. The creatures were so grateful to get a second crack at life. I felt generous.

One by one, I tossed out the chicken necks we had used as bait.

We then set off north across the mud flats to Crab Jack's hut, dragging the boat behind us. It was a long hike. Ippy limped on his bandaged foot, but he never complained.

As we drew closer to the bay, I felt eyes on me. Instinct told me I was being watched. When we came within sight of Crab Jack's house, I understood. The old sea captain was standing on his covered porch, watching us through his spyglass.

"Ahoy, mates!" he cried, waving at us. We dropped the boat on the sand and ran up the wooden steps. Guessing we'd be thirsty, he handed us lemonades. We gulped them down greedily.

You should see his house. It's an old fishing shack. It's covered in shells, shark jaws, old fishing tackle, giant anchors, lifesavers, driftwood, and lots of other stuff Crab Jack has scrounged up on the beach. That's how he got his name—he's a beachcomber, just like a crab.

He combs the beach looking for treasure. Once he took my buddies and me midway down the island to Three Trees. Under those palms is where the pirate Jean Lafitte is said to have buried his sea chest. We dug and dug with picks and shovels, but never unearthed any gold coins. Many years ago, though, Crab Jack found a silver coin with the date 1812. Since then he's never missed a day hunting treasure.

"You never know," he's fond of saying. "Today could be my lucky day."

Crab Jack was thrilled to help repair the hole in the rowboat. He loves boats and hates to see one wounded. "Haul it over there," he said, pointing to two saw-horses. We lifted it up. After a careful examination, he went to work. With skillful hands, he replaced old boards with new and sealed leaks with tar.

While Crab Jack worked, Ippy and I talked. We decided to paint our boat yellow and name her the "Sailor Moon." Crab Jack said we could keep it at his place. Then he looked down and saw the fresh scars on Ippy's foot.

At first he was playful. "Get your foot caught in the spokes of that special delivery bike?" he teased Ippy. Ippy was caught off guard. He did not know what to say. He did not want to lie; yet Samson had sworn us both to silence. We just stood there, dumbfounded.

"What's the matter?" asked Crab Jack. "Cat got both your tongues?" Ippy and I excused ourselves and ducked under the house for a quick powwow. Was it safe to tell Crab Jack about the shark attack? After all, wasn't he virtually a hermit? As far as we knew, he spoke with almost no one in town except for the Ippolitos and the other shrimpers he employed, and certainly never the tourists. We voted to let him in on our secret.

We told him everything. When he heard that Samson warned us not to talk about it, he got boiling mad.

"Blast those foolish landlubbers!" he cursed, hurling his saw through the air. "One day they're going to stick their heads in the sand too far. Then they'll be sorry. The inhabitants of this pretty little island live a charmed life—for now. But, mark my words, mateys: there's a price to pay for living in paradise—and sometimes that price is paid in human lives. By thunder, there *is* danger in the water. Pretending it's not there won't make it go away."

If anyone should know about danger in the water, it's Crab Jack. All his life he has followed the sea. He knows her ways—especially her treacherous ones. In June of 1886, he boarded a ship bound for Venezuela. He shoved off from his homeport of Indianola, just down the coast from Galveston. On that hot summer day, he never guessed he was waving good-bye forever to his wife, their ten-year-old son, and their baby daughter. Two months later, a terrible hurricane hit

Indianola. The Gulf waters covered the little town, drowning its inhabitants. The survivors moved away. Indianola was destroyed and never rebuilt. Crab Jack never saw his family again.

And—now get this—on the very day that Crab Jack's family died—August 20, 1886—my sainted mother died, too, giving birth to me.

Sunday, May 20, 1900

I met a girl today who is as beautiful as Venus. Meeting Daisy almost makes up for my missing the opening day of baseball season. This afternoon the Houston Mud Cats played our hometown team, Weber's All-Professionals. It seems everyone in the city turned out to rally our boys to victory except Ippy and me. I'm not supposed to go to games on the Sabbath. Ippy could have gone, but he chose to stay with me. Ever since he realized that it was me who rescued him from that shark, he has stuck to me like glue. He says he owes me his life.

I guess now I owe him something, too. Because if it hadn't been for him, I wouldn't have met Daisy. This is how it happened. It was late afternoon. Ippy and I were lazing around on my front porch, watching the waves crash onto the beach. We could hear the fans cheering over at Beach Park. Suddenly Ippy sat up and announced that he was hungry. I went inside and poked around in the pantry, but nothing I suggested pleased him.

"Not just anything will do," he said. "I want something sweet and juicy." He paused, then he clicked his fingers. "I've got it," he said. "Follow me." He jumped on his bike and headed north on Twenty-fifth Street. I was right behind him.

The streets were deserted. We crossed Broadway, making a quick right into the alley behind it. Ippy motioned for me to pull over. We got off our bikes and quietly walked them. The alley ran behind the mansions of Millionaire's Row. After a couple of hundred yards, we passed behind an elegant three-story brick mansion.

Along the back of this particular property was a peach orchard. A cast-iron fence separated us from the fruit trees, but some of their branches hung over into the alley. These overhanging branches were so heavy with fruit that they almost brushed the ground. Dozens of peaches had fallen into the alley. There they lay, rotting among the oyster shells, smushed by buggy wheels and eaten by worms and birds.

Ippy wanted to pick the fruit from the overhanging branches. "It'll waste if we don't!" he argued. He had a good point, but instinct whispered in my ear: "That fruit is private property." What we were planning to do boiled down to a raid.

I debated what to do. Looking back, I know now that I wasn't in a good frame of mind for making decisions. I was sore about the Sabbath. All of Ippy's talk about eating something cold and sweet had made my mouth water, too. Also, I knew that nobody would catch us since everyone was at the game. I convinced myself that I would actually be doing a good deed by eating the fruit. After all, wouldn't it be wrong to let it waste? And wasn't the fruit technically in the alley? I knew then how Adam felt when Eve offered him the apple. My resolve to always do the right thing weakened. I gave in. We picked the fruit.

We sat down against the fence and proceeded to eat. We ate peaches until our fingers and mouths were dripping with the sticky-sweet juice and our stomachs were swollen.

When we were done, we each had a good-sized pile of peach pits. It was Ippy who threw the first one. What was I to do? Of course I had to get him back. So I threw a pit at him. Then he had to get me back, so he threw one.

We went on like this for some time, running up and down the alley, throwing peach pits at each other, doubling over with laughter, until we heard someone cry, "OWWW!" It was a girl's voice. I must have beaned her with a peach pit. The voice had come from with the yard with the peach orchard. Ippy and I climbed over the fence to investigate. Now we were trespassing, too.

A brick footpath, carpeted in velvety moss, led us through the shady orchard. Had we continued on, the path would have taken us straight across a sunny lawn and into a flower garden. In the center of the garden was a goldfish pond. A statue of a naked boy stood in the middle. He was on tiptoe, forever pouring a jug of water onto the little fishes below. The fountain made a pleasant, almost musical, sound. Directly behind this garden sat the house.

On any other day, I would have been in awe of the house's grandeur, for both it and the garden were truly magnificent. But given our circumstances, I was more interested in its windows. A bank of six windows ran the length of each of the three floors, and every blasted one of the eighteen faced the backyard. The windows were as tall as a man and opened outward like doors.

On the top two floors, some of them were propped open onto the balconies. Anyone inside could both see and hear what went on out back.

Ippy and I were considering what to do next when we heard a second cry from my victim. "Over here," she called. The voice came from somewhere to our right. We tramped through the orchard. In the far corner of the yard was a chinaberry tree. Lying at its base were two black boots and two black stockings. We looked up to see two bare feet, dangling from a low limb. We had found our girl.

She was lovely to behold. Her chestnut brown hair was not pinned up on top of her head in the usual fashion. She had allowed it to fall loose. It encircled her shoulders and cascaded in gentle waves down her back. In her lap was an open book.

"Hello," she called out, quite friendly. She dabbed her forehead. There was blood on the hankie.

"Oh, no," I cried. "You're hurt."

"Oh, fiddlesticks," she said, laughing. "Don't be silly. I'm just fine. It's just a little blood. See?" She held up the hankie for inspection. Still, I wanted a good look for myself. I offered to help her down from the tree, but she didn't need any help. She slid down the trunk and landed between Ippy and me.

She seemed steady on her feet, but I thought it best that she sit for a while. I escorted her to a bench in the rose garden. I examined her forehead. Sure enough, my peach pit had dented it, but it will heal just fine.

We got to talking. I apologized to her for stealing her fruit. She wasn't angry, she said. She had enjoyed spying on our "little mischief," as she called it. I blushed red.

Ippy must have wandered off about then, but she and I sat side-by-side among the roses, getting along like a house on fire, for a big chunk of the afternoon. She told me her name is Daisy Larchmont and that she's thirteen years old. I've never seen her at school because she attends the Ursuline Catholic convent school. That's five blocks from my house. She loves Shakespeare as much as I, and *Romeo and Juliet* is her favorite play.

Daisy doesn't have any sisters or brothers yet, but her mother is expecting a child in September. Daisy and her mother sail to France every June to study painting. But this summer they'll stay on the island. Her mother's condition is very delicate. She's already suffered three miscarriages, so the doctors have forbidden her to travel.

All too soon, a maid appeared on the third-floor balcony, calling Daisy in to practice the piano. "Oh," Daisy exclaimed. "That's Flossie—she's French you know." And with that she ran across the green lawn, disappeared into her palace, and vanished from my life.

Daisy has a smile that makes my heart turn somersaults and eyes as green as the ocean. You know, a funny thing just occurred to me. Here it is bedtime and I don't even know who won today's ballgame. I wonder what book Daisy was reading? I wish I could just ring her up and ask. Maybe she's already asleep. I've never been less sleepy in my life—I can't stop thinking about her.

Thursday, May 31, 1900

Yesterday my drama club at Ball High School performed for a women's group called the Wednesday Club. The Wednesday Club meets every other week from October through May to improve their minds through art and literature. The club president is Mrs. Magnolia Larchmont—Daisy's mother. And—are you ready for this?—because this was their last meeting of the year, they met at Daisy's house instead of their headquarters on Market Street.

We thespians arrived at the Broadway entrance of Larchmont Hall about 3:30 P.M. Two winged lions guard the front steps leading up to the gigantic mansion. I'll bet the house sits a full twelve feet above street level. I counted eighteen steps before we reached the porch. Was I surprised when Samson's brother, Moses, answered the door. He must be the footman. He led us into a grand reception hall. A two-story curved wooden staircase takes up most of that room. We waited there while the twenty-five women wound up the business portion of their meeting. When it was almost time for our program to begin, we were ushered into a large parlor called the Gold Room. And there was Daisy.

We took our seats just as Mrs. Larchmont finished addressing the Wednesday Club. "Ladies, I leave you with this shocking truth," she said. "As we speak, there are naked walls in the schools and homes of our very city!" On these walls, she proposed, should hang paintings by Rubens, Rembrandt, and Gainsborough. "Only then," she continued, "can the eye be trained to appreciate true beauty." She suggested that the Wednesday Club create a traveling picture gallery.

I was to perform first. I guess I'm a bit of a ham because I love speaking in public. Momsie says I'll make a great lawyer. I cleared my throat and recited that famous soliloquy from *Hamlet*: "To be, or not to be: that is the question: / Whether 'tis nobler in the mind to suffer . . ." The women clapped enthusiastically when I was done.

After Caroline Bright concluded our program by singing "Beware," Mrs. Larchmont asked Daisy to play a piano sonata by Beethoven. She plays beautifully. Then Moses announced that refreshments were served on the back lawn. We sat at tables covered in pink linen and ate ice cream and strawberries from silver bonbon dishes.

Before I knew it, it was 5:00—time to go. Not once did I get to speak to Daisy alone. She smiled at me twice, though, and Moses slipped me her telephone number.

Sunday, June 3, 1900

Since school's been out, it's been kind of quiet around here. All but three of the medical students have taken the train back home. They packed up those funny-smelling specimen jars they kept on their dressers. What are those mushy red and pink things floating around in those jars, anyway? They look like dead frogs, only without the skin.

A few people have stopped by the house to inquire about the classified ad I put in the paper. Hopefully, by week's end, we'll have rented out the three empty upstairs rooms. Here's the ad:

Large, airy south room, sleeps 6, handsomely furnished, $15 a month, also 2 small but cozy west rooms, $12 a month. Light housekeeping with table board. Close to beach. References required. Q½ and 25th Streets.

Ippy and I went over to Crab Jack's last week. We painted the *Sailor Moon*. Then, on Saturday, Willie, Frank, Al, Ippy, and I took her out on the "high seas" for her maiden voyage. Fargo came, too. He loves boating.

We rowed over to Bolivar Point, where I spotted some seagulls circling over the water. They kept diving, hitting the water, and catching shrimp. An oily film coated the water. The air smelled like watermelon. I had a hunch that, beneath those shrimp, trout were feeding. The signs were strong. "Cast your line," my instinct commanded. No sooner had my line hit the water than I hooked a fish! We all went home with stringers full of speckled trout.

I told Samson about Daisy. Although he doesn't know her, he knows a lot about life at Larchmont Hall. He hears gossip from his brother, Moses, because he works there.

Moses looks dashing in his royal blue and gold livery (that's what Mrs. Larchmont calls his footman uniform), especially because he's over six feet tall. Among his other duties, he prepares afternoon tea for "Milady" and accompanies her downtown when she goes shopping. Heads really turn when Mrs. Larchmont walks down Market Street, Moses trailing behind her, carrying her mountain of packages.

According to Samson, Daisy's father, Cornelius Albert Larchmont II, is a very important man. He owns railroads and banks and cotton presses and steamships. He's a millionaire many times over. I was disappointed to learn that he owned the textile mill that shut down, the one where Ippy's family worked two years ago. Could someone as wonderful as Daisy have a father who cares so little about the misery of others?

Mr. Larchmont likes opera—and opera singers, too, apparently. In the last year he has taken it upon himself to launch the career of a young and promising singer from Italy named Lili Patti. He's paying for her voice lessons and has installed her in a fancy suite at the

Hotel Grand. "Strictly business," he claims. Some nights, though, Mr. Larchmont doesn't come home for supper—and according to Moses, it's not because he's working late at the Cotton Exchange.

Poor Mrs. Larchmont. And here she is expecting a baby, too. What will happen when the baby comes, I wonder? Moses told Samson that Mr. Larchmont has always wanted a son to take over his business.

Friday, June 8, 1900

Our worries are over. We're full up. As of yesterday, all five upstairs rooms are rented. On Wednesday afternoon, a woman named Mrs. Newton and her three kids arrived on the train from St. Louis. Mrs. Newton has gorgeous orange-red hair. She and her family are fleeing summer in the big city. They've rented the large south room. Mr. Newton will come down for a holiday when he can. Mrs. Newton and the kids will stay on until the week of Labor Day. She paid Momsie the entire three-month rent in advance.

Later that same day, two elderly gentlemen with binoculars slung around their necks rented the rear west room. They're birdwatchers. Then, yesterday, some honeymooners rented the remaining west room. Since check-in, sightings of those lovebirds have been rare indeed. They only leave their room for meals.

Of course, Mr. Plummer and the three medical students who stayed still have the two east rooms. I pray that the Newton kids—twin six-year-old boys and a baby girl—are well behaved. Mr. Plummer cherishes his peace and quiet. We can't let the summer people run off our number one roomer.

Tuesday, June 12, 1900

I just got back from meeting the guys for our Tuesday afternoon swim and hotdog at Murdoch's Pier and Bath House. But today I brought along the Newton twins, Henry and Harold. I call them Hank and Hal. Mrs. Newton was nervous about letting her boys swim in the Gulf. "Don't go past the first ropes," she shouted at us from the upstairs balcony as we walked down Twenty-fifth Street toward the beach.

At first I wasn't too keen to have two little kids tagging along. It was Momsie's idea. Mrs. Newton's had a hard time of it lately, with her baby sick and all. On top of that, the baby's crying at night hasn't helped matters with Mr. Plummer. He has Tuesday afternoons off. Today being Tuesday, Momsie thought it a good idea to let him enjoy his pipe and newspaper in the sitting room without two six-year-olds underfoot.

As kids go, though, Hank and Hal really aren't too bad. I took them to the souvenir shell shops on the Midway. They're easy to babysit. They could watch sand crabs scuttle along the beach for hours.

Wednesday, June 13, 1900

For almost two weeks, I have been phoning Larchmont Hall to speak to Daisy. It's Flossie who answers the phone—I can tell by her accent—but Daisy is always "out."

So this morning I gave Samson a note for Daisy. He took it to Moses and brought back this note in reply:

> Dear J. T.,
>
> Meet me at Woollam's Lake next Tuesday at 4:00 P.M.
>
> > Daisy

She wants to see me! How will I make it till Tuesday? *Tuesday!* Why, that's the day I always swim with the guys. Oh, well, missing just this once won't matter—they probably won't even notice I'm not there.

These next six days will feel like an eternity.

Tuesday, June 19, 1900

Today I was supposed to meet Daisy at 4:00. I finished my afternoon chores in doubletime. Wouldn't you know it though—just as I was set to run out the door and catch the West Broadway trolley to Woollam's Lake, the telephone rang. It was from the mother superior at St. Mary's. A water pipe had burst, flooding the entire first floor of the orphanage. Momsie asked us to help out. Samson hitched our mule, Bessie, to the wagon; I loaded the tools; and we rode off west down the beach.

When 4:00 rolled around, we were still at St. Mary's. We'd fixed the broken pipe, but Samson decided we should mop the floor. It was a quarter to five when he finally dropped me off at the lake. I had thirty minutes to find Daisy before I had to head home to help with the supper. Woollam's Lake is a huge park. I had no idea when or where I'd find her.

I raced along the garden paths but no Daisy. I ran along the water's edge, searching the faces in the canoes, but still no Daisy. I was almost out of time and definitely out of breath when I spotted her.

She was standing on a bridge. Her gown was white and flowing. With her long and graceful neck, she looked like one of the swans floating in the pond below. I sighed.

"Daisy!" I cried. Yet she did not move. She did not speak. She stayed frozen. And yet I knew that she had both seen me and heard me. Was she that mad at my lateness?

I moved a little closer. Then I could see. A few feet away under some live oaks an artist stood in front of an easel. He was painting Daisy's portrait. On a bench nearby sat Flossie, cajoling "Mademoiselle" not to fidget.

The artist saw me and called for a short break. He lit a cigar. Daisy and I took a stroll. Flossie stayed right on our heels, snooping. I don't like her. I loaned Daisy one of Popeye's old poetry books. I had dogeared the page of my favorite poem by Robert Burns:

> O, my Luve's like a red red rose
> That's newly sprung in June . . .

Tuesday, June 26, 1900

This afternoon Momsie shooed Hank, Hal, and me out of the house for our swim. We waited at Murdoch's, but none of the other guys showed up. How strange. Even if Ippy had to work late, Willie, Al, and Frank certainly could have come.

I've received no notes from Daisy, though I've sent one every day for the past week.

Thursday, June 28, 1900

I set up a croquet game in the backyard this morning, hoping that some of the guys might drop by and want to play. But it ended up being just Hank, Hal, and me hitting balls with mallets.

Still no word from Daisy. I'm beginning to feel like a leper.

Saturday, June 30, 1900

I wasn't imagining it. I haven't been able to find the guys anywhere, but when I took Hank and Hal to the roller rink today, guess who we saw skating? Ippy, Al, Willie, and Frank. And that's not all. Daisy was there, too—on the arm of some prep school guy named Putty Brighton.

To make matters worse, when we skated towards the guys, they just raced away. I tried not to show I cared, but once I got home, all I wanted to do was hole up here in my bedroom. I felt like I didn't have a friend in the world. Shortly afterward, I heard a knock at my door. Samson entered with two frosty goblets of Momsie's sugar mint tea. Fargo spotted the open door and charged in. I made room for the two of them on my cot (I had to lift Fargo up). I began to feel better having two buddies in my room. I told Samson everything.

Samson is very wise. He says Ippy and the guys are still my friends. They're just sore because I skipped our Tuesday swim to meet Daisy in the park. I guess that was pretty awful of me, picking her over them. I really need these guys. I can fix this problem.

However, the situation with Daisy cannot be fixed. Samson's brother, Moses, revealed why Daisy is not answering my letters. Her French maid told Mrs. Larchmont about our meeting at Woollam's Lake.

"So? What's wrong with that?" I asked Samson. "It is certainly acceptable for two chaperoned teenagers to stroll in a public park."

Samson thought long and hard before speaking. "J. T.," he said, "what I have to tell you is not easy." He says Mrs. Larchmont is a big snob. Because Momsie runs a boardinghouse, Mrs. Larchmont does not consider us to be social equals. Therefore, she does not think I am an acceptable suitor for Daisy. She has forbidden Daisy to have anything more to do with me. She wants Daisy to marry a rich guy like Putty Brighton.

"Why, the nerve! I was born on this island and so were my father and grandfather! Doesn't that count for something?" I cried. "And besides, I'll give Daisy the best life imaginable. I'll make gobs of money as a lawyer. Daisy's my girl. If I have to, I'll fight for her."

"But, J. T., that's the last thing you should do," said Samson. "Mrs. Larchmont will just find other ways to stop you. Don't underestimate her. You know that upcoming charity luncheon for St. Mary's orphanage? How Momsie's had her heart set on running the lemonade table? Mrs. Larchmont is head of the refreshment committee. She has stricken Momsie's name from the list of volunteers."

I couldn't believe my ears. Momsie will be crushed. For years she has poured her heart into helping the orphanage. And, now, to be banished by Mrs. Larchmont?

Mrs. Larchmont must be ruthless. I'm angry, but ashamed, too. Poor Momsie. Somehow I must forget Daisy.

Thursday, July 5, 1900

Yesterday Hal disappeared. It was the Fourth of July. After watching a parade and listening to speeches, some of us went over to the Garten Verein (Garden Club) for a picnic. As I spread our quilt on the grass, I could see the Ursuline Academy through the palms. My heart sank as I thought of Daisy.

A German oompah band was playing marching music at the pavilion. We were all wearing red, white, and blue. Momsie and Mrs. Newton began laying out the fried chicken lunch. Mr. Plummer knew we were thirsty, so he was hailing a waiter with a tray of cold drinks. The medical students wanted to bowl a few rounds before dinner. Samson was off somewhere tying up Bessie with the wagon. I was pushing Hank and Hal on the swings.

Everything was going smoothly until the baby started crying. Momsie needed Mrs. Newton to help with lunch, so I tended to the baby. I left the boys just long enough to give the baby a bottle and move her buggy into the shade. By the time I returned to the play-ground, Hank was waiting on the seesaw, but Hal was nowhere in sight.

Mrs. Newton almost fainted when she heard the news. "Oh, my poor, poor boy is lost!" she cried. Mr. Plummer surprised me by offering to watch Hank while I scoured the park for Hal. After checking everywhere —the dance floor, the tennis courts, the bowling greens—I still could not find him. I began to worry. What if he had left the park?

Just when things were looking their worst, up walked Ippy, Willie, Al, and Frank. And who were they leading by the hand? None other than Hal. They had run into him at the zoo. When they spotted him all by himself, they realized something was fishy.

What an oddly wonderful day. Once we were face to face, the guys just couldn't stay sore. Isn't it funny how good things can come of bad?

Saturday, July 21, 1900

Ippy and I were nearly killed today. We were rowing out to Red Fish Bay when two yachts began racing to-ward us at a fast clip. At first we weren't alarmed. We assumed they would give us the right of way. But they just kept coming straight toward us.

We rowed as though our life depended upon it—and it did. We got out of the way moments before one of the sailboats would have sliced us in two. It didn't even swerve to miss us. As the boat whizzed past, one of the sailors looked over at us and let out a mean laugh. It was that prep school fellow, Putty Brighton.

And this is the guy Mrs. Larchmont wants Daisy to marry? The town playboy?

Monday, August 20, 1900

My fourteenth birthday

I can think of better ways to celebrate my birthday. First thing this morning I opened the newspaper only to read:

> Daisy Larchmont, the daughter of Cornelius and Magnolia Larchmont, has been seen lately in the company of Mr. Patrick ("Putty") Brighton, the son of Reginald and Harriet Brighton. Ladies and gentlemen of Galves- ton, are those wedding bells we're hearing?

Ugh.

After supper, Momsie brought out a chocolate cake and everyone sang "Happy Birthday" to me. I got some great gifts, but my favorite is from Momsie. It's a full-length rain slicker. She ordered it from the Sears, Roebuck & Co. catalog. It is guaranteed to be 100% waterproof. It has automatic buckles and large outside pockets with heavy flaps. I feel just like a fireman when I put it on.

I sure needed a new rain coat. My old yellow one is three inches too short in the sleeves!

Tuesday, August 21, 1900

Earlier, when I went out to meet the milkman, I saw a flash of red behind the fig tree where I stash my bicycle. I ran over to investigate. Taped to the handlebars, I found a letter and a red rose. The letter said:

> Dear J. T.,
>
> *Don't believe everything you read in the newspaper.*
> *Happy (Belated) Birthday!*
>
> *Daisy*

My love is like a red, red rose . . .

Wow. She does care.

Monday, August 27, 1900

On Saturday, when September rolls around, the summer people will leave town. Momsie calls this time "fruit basket turnover." Once again, the west and south rooms will become vacant. In a couple of weeks, however, the medical students will return for the fall semester and fill them back up again. Momsie is already anticipating the return of "her boys." She's stocking up on coffee beans, cases of root beer, and lightbulbs. Medical students do a lot of late-night studying.

It has become harder and harder to keep the twins out of Mr. Plummer's hair. Usually when he comes in from work, I let him have the sitting room to himself. The boys and I head out back to toss the football. But lately it's just too hot to be outside. I wish I felt comfortable taking them down to the Gulf for a swim, but a big and dangerous surf has been piling in. The undertow is so strong, I fear it will suck the both of them under. Momsie knows it's been tough on me. She reminds me that the Newtons return to St. Louis on Saturday, the eighth.

I am actually looking forward to school starting in a few weeks. Maybe it will keep my mind off Daisy.

Tuesday, September 4, 1900

Morning

At about 4:00 this morning, a deafening clap of thunder awakened me from a deep sleep. A violent storm had come out of the Gulf of Mexico. I tried to flip on my desk lamp, but lightning must have knocked out the power. I fumbled on the pantry shelves for a candle, a lantern, or a match, but I could find no light to guide me. I had to grope my way along the dark hallway to get to the front porch.

Once outside, I could hear the roar of the breakers crashing on the beach, but I could not see them. Both the city and the sea were cloaked in darkness. Sometimes forks of lightning flashed, brightening the night sky for an instant. Then I could see the heavy rain pummeling the waves, turning them angry and foamy.

Later

Ippy called. He'd been to deliver a telegram to the Weather Bureau office over at the E. S. Levy Building.

He said that the storm we had this morning came from the direction of Cuba. He also said that another tropical storm was moving northward over Cuba.

Ippy asked one of the weathermen in the bureau if we islanders should be concerned about the warning. After all, *disturbance* can mean *hurricane.*

But the weatherman was not concerned. Matter of fact, he was downright casual. "Nothing to worry about, young man," he said, slapping Ippy on the back to reassure him. "If a hurricane does develop and it does hit Galveston, the bay will absorb the shock. No hurricane has ever destroyed this island. That only happens to towns on the mainland. You've heard about the hurricane of '86? It destroyed the town of Indianola— because it was on the mainland. Yet that same hurricane only dumped a little water on Galveston. Whatever happens, we'll be fine," he concluded, taking a handkerchief from his pocket. He mopped the sweat from his brow. "I, for one, would welcome a good old-fashioned hurricane. It would give us a needed break from this gosh-durned heat," he said. This made the other men in the office laugh.

Ippy thinks the weatherman makes sense, but I don't know. My antennae are up; Momsie was sure right about my instinct. Twice today I've heard *Cuba* and *storm* in the same sentence.

Thursday, September 6, 1900

I didn't need instinct to tell me that the redfish were running today. I could stand on the dock and see for myself. Schools of them were swimming right below the surface of the bay water, tailing it to the Gulf to spawn.

I've never seen the bay so brimful of water. It looks like a giant bathtub about ready to overflow. I guess it's from all the rain we've had. The tides are running so high, they're sloshing up on the docks. That's odd. There's no wind to cause them to be so high.

It was after supper I noticed it, when I'd ridden over to Crab Jack's to fish. When school starts back up and the medical students return, I won't have many of these free nights. Until then, I'm determined to enjoy every single one of them.

Ippy was to join us fishing when he got off work. Since the shark attack, Ippy has not been eager to get back into the water. So, before he arrived, Crab Jack and I waded through the shallows, dragging a net. We caught some piggy perch and croaker for bait.

The fish were starting to bite when Ippy finally rode up. He threw his delivery bike on the sand and joined us on the dock. He was dripping with sweat.

"Sorry I'm late, guys," he said, trying to catch his breath, "but those weathermen just ran me ragged today. All afternoon I did nothing but carry telegrams back and forth between the Western Union office and the Weather Bureau." He grabbed a pole. "You remember that tropical storm that hit Cuba on Tuesday?" he asked, looking at me.

"Yeah . . . ," I said.

"Well, today it went and smashed through Florida," he said.

"Holy mackerel!" I said. "Is it coming toward us?" There's nothing I love better than a good storm."

Ippy shook his head. "No, the weather fellows say it's leaving the Gulf. They predict it will head north and go into the Atlantic."

"Oh, poppycock!" shouted Crab Jack. "What do them swabs know about the sea? Aye, there's a storm a-comin', all right. Just look at them birds," he said, pointing to the western sky.

To the west, high above the downtown area, a flock of seagulls was circling. As we watched, other birds flew over and joined the movement. Ippy and I gulped.

This was indeed a bad omen. It meant nasty weather was coming.

Crab Jack lit his pipe, tossing the match into the water. A redfish swam up and nibbled at it. "Mateys," he said, "would you like to know how I know when a storm's a-comin'?"

"Yes, sir!" we said, at once.

"Well, they don't call me Crab Jack for nothing," he said, chuckling at his own joke. He took a long puff on his pipe. "I watch them crabs. Crabs is mighty queer critters, you know. When a storm's a-comin', they head for deep water and bury themselves in the mud. They won't come back, neither, until that storm is good and gone. Why, back before the hurricane of '75, I couldn't get no crabs—except for one little old muddy thing. That storm didn't catch Crab Jack neither. I pulled up my nets and went ashore."

At just that moment, something big tugged on Ippy's line. We went back to fishing and forgot all about the storm.

Later on, though, before we headed home with stringers of redfish, Ippy and I remembered the warning from the seagulls. We dragged *Sailor Moon* off the bay shore. With Crab Jack's help, we hoisted her up and tied her to the beams beneath his shack. We wanted her safe, just in case that storm did turn our way.

Friday, September 7, 1900

I saw Daisy this evening. I've seen her almost every Friday lately. That's when she swims in the Gulf. She loves to bathe in the surf at dusk. Daisy tries to stay out of the sun. It would scorch her fair skin.

I'd give anything to swim with her, but her mother says I can't. But there's no law that says I can't watch her swim. So, on Friday nights, I spy on Daisy from Murdoch's Pier.

After washing the supper dishes, I head for the pier. I take the stairs to the upper deck. Leaning on the railing, I scan the beach for a carriage stamped with the Larchmont coat of arms.

When her carriage finally arrives, I hold my breath until she steps out and onto the sand. Trailing right behind her, every time, is that nosy French maid, carrying stacks of towels and clothes. The two of them duck into one of those little bathhouses on wheels that are parked at the water's edge.

It's always the same. After a bit, the bathhouse door swings open and Daisy steps out in her swimsuit. As she walks down the steps into the water, she stuffs her hair into a bathing cap. She wades through the warm, green water. As waves rise and curl before her, she tucks her head and dives into one. The wave breaks with her in it and floats her back to shore.

But this evening was different from the others. Daisy didn't go swimming. She took one look at the Gulf of Mexico and drove off. The waves were too rough. All the sand they were kicking up had turned them an ugly brown. The wind whipped the waves so high that they reached up and touched Murdoch's lamps that hang over the water. By nightfall the beach is usually packed with bathers. But there was no swimming tonight. The beach was deserted.

With Daisy gone so early, I had some time to kill. I went for a stroll along the water's edge. The tide was way up on the beach. A bright moon blazed a path for me. I was surprised to find myself truly alone. No sandpipers chased minnows in the tide. No crabs disappeared down holes in the sand. The beach was completely deserted. Everyone and everything had fled from the strong wind and waves. Crab Jack was right. That storm was a-comin'.

I hurried home to tell Mr. Plummer about the giant breakers and the missing crabs. He said that he, too, knew a storm was coming. On his way home from work, he had spotted two warning flags flying atop the Weather Bureau building. Those flags alerted us to a powerful storm approaching from the northeast.

When Momsie heard this, she smiled. She was knitting and rocking back and forth in her chair. "That's good news," she said. "We could use a good overflow. Just think, J. T., how good that cool air is going to feel tomorrow. It's been a murderously hot summer."

I nodded heartily in agreement as I headed for my diary and my cot. Come what may, I love the delicious threat of a good storm.

Sunday, September 9, 1900

Midmorning

We awoke to the pealing of bells at the Ursuline Convent. I am shaken and beaten like the hundreds of others who took refuge here in this chapel last night. What a night of horrors! I cannot believe we survived it.

Sunlight is streaming through the two-story arched windows, bouncing off the multicolored stone and brick, blinding us with its garish brilliance. The sky outside is shockingly clear and blue. It seems sinister for such a beautiful day to follow such an ugly night.

The city is covered in water. Momsie says I cannot go out until the water goes down. While I wait, I will use this time to write in my diary. I will try to record the events of the last thirty-odd hours as faithfully as I can.

*What happened yesterday, Saturday,
September 8, 1900*

Dawn

I was at home, sleeping in my old bed. I was dreaming I had gone back in time. The year was 1528. I was exploring the Texas coast with Cabeza de Vaca. We were in a terrible hurricane off Galveston Island. The wind and rain had shredded our clothes. We were wet, half-naked, and shivering with cold. With blistered hands, we gripped our oars and rowed hard toward shore.

We were exhausted. We rowed and rowed toward the island, yet we never could get close enough to land. Great waves crashed over our boats, pushing us back out to sea, washing our men overboard and drowning them. Each wave was bigger than the one before. One by one, our boats went down. Soon only de Vaca and I were left.

Then a single roll of the sea capsized our boat. We were tossed into the rushing surf. Hours later, we washed onto the beach, half-drowned. After several days, we recovered and made a life for ourselves on the flat and sandy island. But de Vaca never trusted our island. He named it Malhado, meaning Island of —

I awoke with a start. Whew! I thought. What a nightmare. My heart was pounding. My pillow was soaked with sweat. I looked at my alarm clock: 6:00. Good, I thought. Soon it will be light outside. I needed some fresh air to shake off the dream. I threw on my robe and walked to the front porch.

When I opened the front door, a blast of chilly wind hit me in the face. A light rain was falling. To my left, I could see the sun peeking over the horizon. As it grew lighter, I could see more around me. Water was standing in our street ankle-deep. Had that much rain already fallen? I wondered. I crept down the stairs to find out.

I stuck my finger in the water and tasted it. It was salty. This was no rainwater. While I had slept, my neighborhood had become part of the Gulf of Mexico.

It's a good thing our house sits so high off the ground or I might be worried about such rapidly rising water. Popeye knew what he was doing when he built this house. It's rock solid. The lot is five feet above sea level, and the house is raised another eight feet above that. I can walk underneath it, it's so tall.

Midmorning

When I went back into the house, Samson was puttering around the kitchen, frying bacon and eggs and perking coffee. I started on the lunches. So few people were rooming with us right then that I had to make only three and a half sacks. Mr. Plummer didn't need one because he comes home for Saturday lunch. The lunches were for the Newtons. Today they were supposed to board a train bound for Houston. Mr. Newton was to meet them there, and then they'd all go back to St. Louis.

We were all excited about the coming storm. Over breakfast we huddled around Mr. Plummer, who read us weather updates. *The Galveston Daily News* had not just one but five scattered references to the storm. On page two, we learned that a storm had hit Florida. The second item was one sentence long and appeared on page three, describing how the storm was raging along the Gulf Coast. The other three articles downplayed the possibility of a storm, predicting only "local rains Saturday and Sunday; variable winds." We were more confused than ever after having read them all. We did not know what to expect. According to the newspaper, we were in for nothing we hadn't had before—some wind and some rain but little else.

But I wasn't satisfied. That dream had rattled me. If a bad storm was coming, I wanted to know so we could prepare. I decided to call the Weather Bureau to find out. The chief of the department himself, Isaac Cline, answered the phone.

"This storm is nothing to worry about, son." He said he'd been tracking this storm since Tuesday. "Just expect a little water and a lot of wind." He told me that he had warned downtown shopkeepers to raise their goods three feet off the ground because of flooding. I thanked him kindly and hung up the phone. I could quit worrying.

Mostly it seemed like any other Saturday. Samson and I cleared the breakfast dishes from the table. Momsie had popped a veal rump roast into the oven and was stirring cake batter. Mr. Plummer pulled on his black knee-high rubber boots and waded off to catch the streetcar for work at the printing company downtown. The only thing different about this Saturday was that Mrs. Newton didn't take the kids to the beach. Instead, she went up to her room to finish packing their trunks for St. Louis.

I stood at the sink, scrubbing plates, listening to the rain. The breeze had cooled down the kitchen some. The window above the sink gave me a great view west.

The water in the streets was rising rapidly. What was once a trickle was now a brown stream rushing through the deep gutters. Some neighborhood kids were sailing toy boats and splashing each other. They were soaking wet. I could hear them laughing. I could also hear Hank and Hal in the front room. They had been begging their mother to let them go outside and play in the rain.

I finished the dishes, dried my hands, and went into the sitting room. I offered to take the boys outside. They jumped up and down for joy. Without waiting for their mother's okay, they stripped off their boots and stockings and dashed out the door into the rain. I threw on my old rain slicker since I was going to get muddy. I had to run to catch up with the twins.

Soon Samson appeared carrying an old beat-up washtub. He helped Hal inside it and sent him floating down the watery street. Meanwhile, Hank and a buddy were rigging up a homemade raft and trying it out. A few ladies were wading in the shallow water. And, for some crazy reason, thousands of tiny frogs were hopping everywhere. Everyone was in a holiday mood. What fun.

Late morning

All of a sudden, the sky began to look dangerous. It got very dark. The wind was up. Low clouds raced across the black sky. The rain hit us like pebbles. Although I had not seen any lightning, I thought it best to get the boys out of harm's way. We raced for shelter.

I hustled them up the back way and onto the porch. They were too muddy to go in the front door. They hated to have to go inside with their friends still out. I thought some licorice sticks might cheer them up. I went inside to get a couple and ran into Mrs. Newton in the hall. She had been expecting us. In her arms were towels and fresh clothes for the boys. I could hear their bath water running.

With the twins taken care of, I walked to the front porch to watch the storm. In just a short time, the river that was once Twenty-fifth Street had grown wider and deeper. All kinds of interesting things floated in it. Squares of wood, boxes, toys, barrels, horse dung, snakes, and toads, toads, and more toads joined the rushing stream.

The water had washed over the sidewalks and invaded some yards. What a shame, I thought, as I watched the brown water ruin Mrs. Wood's prized rose garden. I thought how fortunate it was that most houses on the island are raised on stilts and well above the ground.

Big groups of people passed by my house on their way to the beach. A heavy sea was running in the Gulf, they shouted. They wanted a closer look at the sea. I, too, was itching to see it and wanted to join them. I worried that the storm would pass before I could see the wild waves, and suspected that Al, Willie, and Frank were down at the beach already. Perhaps I'd run into them and we could have a party. We could split an order of boiled clams at a little restaurant on the Midway and celebrate the storm. I knew Ippy couldn't join us. He always works Saturdays.

I grabbed an umbrella, joined the throng, and waded the three blocks to the beach. The rain came down in giant splashes now. It stung like hail. At first, I raised my umbrella as a shield, but as I waded across R½ Street, a big gust of wind hit. It picked up my umbrella and me with it. For a few seconds I was airborne. Then the wind snapped the umbrella spines backward. It sucked the cloth clean off the spines and carried it off into the air. Plop! I fell into the water. I felt like a fool with my dirty bottom, holding a naked metal stick. The rain pelted me in the face. I threw the useless umbrella into the muddy water. As I was already wet through, it didn't make any difference.

At the beach I found a huge crowd gathered. Some wore bathing suits. They had their backs to me. They were staring out to sea. Monster waves were breaking over the streetcar trestle that ran out over the Gulf. The streetcar had stopped running because water had covered the tracks.

If I hadn't known any better, I would have guessed that it was the Fourth of July. As if they were watching fireworks, the crowd oohed! and aahed! whenever a really big wave rocketed over the streetcar rails and exploded against the pilings in clouds of white spray.

Everyone was having a high old time. I scanned the crowd for the guys, but didn't see them. I decided to check on the Midway. I was walking that direction when I heard a woman yell, 'Hey, everybody! Look what's happening to Murdoch's!"

I turned to look. The angry gray surf was battering Murdoch's. Wave after wave hammered against the upper decks. I watched in disbelief as the bathhouses and piers began to come apart. Big boards flew through the air. I felt so helpless just standing by, watching Murdoch's destroyed. Little by little, the waves pounded it to splinters. It broke into pieces and slid forever into the sea.

The crowd went silent. We were stunned. Just a little further east, I could see what was happening to the Midway. The waves were picking up the little bathhouses on wheels and dashing them against the little shell and souvenir shops.

Suddenly this storm wasn't fun anymore. I took a long, hard look at the surf. It was then that I realized an awful truth. The tide was running *against the north wind*. In an ordinary storm, a north wind should push the tide back *into the Gulf*. Yet these waves had crept way out of the Gulf. They raged high upon the beach and were flooding the city.

Then, clear as a bell, I heard the voice of instinct. I had learned to listen. "This is no ordinary storm," it said. "This is a hurricane."

A deadly storm was upon us. I hurried back to Momsie's to help secure the house.

12:00 *noon*

The storm was much worse than it had been on my way down to the beach. I had to fight my way back into the city. The north wind had become a powerhouse. It blew in strong gusts, pushing me back. Water stood knee-deep in Twenty-fifth Street and was rising fast. I had to walk against the current. I felt as if my arms and legs moved in slow motion. I thought I'd never make it home. It reminded me of my dream last night, of rowing and rowing, yet never reaching shore.

In just an hour, my flooded street had turned into a raging river. The rushing water bobbed with junk—big junk, now—like tree limbs, lawn chairs, buckets, lampposts, lanterns, fence posts, mailboxes, screen doors, and window shutters. Some of the planks of wood were pretty dangerous, too—they were jagged or had rusty nails sticking out of them. As the big pieces floated toward me, I did a fair job of dodging them. But I guess I got pegged a time or two because, before long, I tasted blood on my lip. It was hard to keep a sharp lookout. I had to squint to see. The rain was icy cold and it stabbed my eyeballs like glass splinters.

Once a doghouse came barreling down the street toward me. A Scottie dog stood in the doorway, chained to the doghouse, barking his head off. That poor thing was so scared. I tried to grab him as he floated past, but I missed. I felt so bad. I hope someone else rescued him.

The wind was really getting worked up. It started howling and throwing a fit. It was tearing the slate shingles off roofs and launching them into the air like deadly missiles. It was knocking down walls and hurling bricks around like grenades.

I put my arms up over my head and leaned against the wind. A man trudged up alongside me, pushing his wife and baby in a bathtub. He said that he lived two blocks from the beach. Water was coming in under his front door. He was moving his family to the highest ground on the island—to Broadway. I looked around me. Other families, too, were carrying their things and heading for the high ground of Broadway. The houses close to the beach were filling with water and some were washing away.

I thanked God for our safe home, so high above the ground. Just then I spied Mr. Plummer rounding the corner and climbing the steps to our front porch. I was never so glad to see anyone in my life. I hurried up the stairs to meet him.

He looked like a drowned rat. As he dumped the water from his boots, he told me how he had walked from downtown because the streetcars had stopped running. Because of high wind and driving rain, the trip had taken him an hour and a half on foot.

"Why didn't you just stay dry and eat lunch at Ritter's?" I asked.

His mouth dropped open at the suggestion. "And leave Mrs. King to battle this hurricane alone?" he replied. "Never!" He was embarrassed to report that many men were doing just that, however, lunching at downtown restaurants because of the rain, although all morning long their wives had been calling their offices, begging them to come home on account of the storm. "Such shameful behavior," he said, shaking his head. He himself had left work as soon as he learned how bad the storm was.

He said downtown was a mess. The strong north wind had pushed the waters of the bay over the wharf and into the streets of the business district. On the Strand he had seen the water in the streets rise up over the three-foot-high curbs and cover the sidewalks. He had seen a man rowing a boat down the street taking someone to Sealy Hospital.

"All railroad tracks and bridges crossing the bay to the mainland are under water. No trains can get out now. The last train to make it out before water covered the tracks left for Houston at 9:00 this morning." He looked me dead in the eye. "J. T.," he said, "do you know what this means?"

I swallowed hard and nodded.

"It means that we are completely cut off from the mainland," he said.

The waters were closing in on us from the bay on the north and the Gulf on the south. We were trapped on the island. There was no escape.

1:00 p.m.

It was good to be inside, out of the storm. My bedroom felt safe and warm and cozy. Soaked and shivering, I peeled off my wet clothes and tugged on dry ones. Famished, I went looking for something hot to eat.

In the sitting room, I found Hank and Hal feeding their sack lunch to Fargo. The baby must have been asleep upstairs. Mrs. Newton was on the phone. She was talking with someone at Western Union. She was sending a telegram to her husband waiting at the station in Houston, explaining their delay. When she finished dictating the message, she handed me the phone.

"It's for you," she said. "It's Ippy."

"Hey, Ippy, old buddy!" I said. "Pretty bad storm, huh?"

"Yup, pretty bad," said Ippy. Then he was strangely silent.

"Hey—is something wrong?" I asked.

"I guess you haven't heard," he said.

"Haven't heard what?" I asked.

"About Mr. Larchmont—Daisy's father!" he said.

"No—what about Mr. Larchmont?" I asked.

"J. T," he said, "he's . . . dead!"

I couldn't believe what I was hearing. "Dead?" I echoed. "How—when—?" I stammered.

"He was eating lunch over at Ritter's," said Ippy, "when the wind started really blowing across the bay. You know how close Ritter's is to the bay, don't you?"

"Yeah, go on," I urged.

"Well, the wind just blew the roof in. Then the beams that hold up everything gave way and the whole building went. The second floor collapsed into the dining room. One of the printing presses upstairs fell on top of Mr. Larchmont, crushing him to death. Some other fellows died, too, they say."

Great Scot! I thought. Those printing presses were from Mr. Plummer's office. If Mr. Plummer had stayed for lunch, he'd be lying dead under a pile of rubble, too.

Poor Mr. Larchmont—dead. And with the new baby on the way.

"Thanks, Buddy, for telling me," I said. "I know things must be crazy there." We hung up. Poor Daisy. I had to find out how she was taking the bad news.

I called Larchmont Hall. Moses answered.

"Gee, Mr. J. T.," he said, "Miss Daisy's not at home. She and Milady are over at Madame Matisse's house. She's their dressmaker. With Mrs. Larchmont in the 'family way,' Madame Matisse has to keep letting out the seams of her dresses so they aren't too tight in the . . ."

I interrupted him. "When are you expecting them back?" I asked.

"Oh, I'm not sure," said Moses, pausing. "Mr. Larchmont has the carriage downtown at Ritter's. He'll pick them up after lunch."

I sucked in my breath. So Moses hadn't heard the bad news yet. I knew I should tell him, but there just wasn't time. Somewhere in the city, Daisy and her mother were waiting for a ride that would never come. It was up to me to rescue them. But first I had to find them.

"Hey, Moses, could you give me Madame Matisse's address?" I asked, trying to sound calm.

"Sure enough," he said, "she's at the corner of Avenue S and Thirty-third, near the beach and across the street from . . ." The next thing I heard was a click. The line had gone dead before he could finish.

Madame Matisse's house was near the beach! Those homes were filling with water. I was in such a hurry to get out the door, I didn't even bother to hang up the phone. I left the receiver dangling by the cord, threw on my yellow rain slicker, and headed for the stable.

I was surprised to find water two feet deep in our yard. I strapped Bessie to the wagon, hopped in the driver's seat, and took the reins. In the blinding wind and stinging rain, I started out for the corner of Avenue S and Thirty-third. I didn't know what I'd find once I got there.

It was crazy outside. The wind was howling like mad. It was ripping up street signs and flinging them into the air like paper kites. With each new gust, the palm trees bent over double. The tall, skinny ones were snapping in two.

As I drove the wagon west along Avenue R, I saw the wind lift a roof off a house like it was tearing off the top of a cereal box. The house then fell in on itself like a house of cards. Glass, shutters, brick, and shingles began flying toward me. I knew I was in terrible danger. Those shingles were as sharp as saw blades.

I threw up my hand to guard my head and shouted, "Look out!" to a man and woman walking in front of me. But they couldn't hear me above all the noise. Shingles hit them in the head and knocked them down. They were swept up by the rushing waters.

I jumped in to save them. I waded through the waist-deep water as fast as I could, but they were too far downstream. In horror, I watched as the waters sucked them under. For what seemed like forever, I just stood staring at where the couple had disappeared. Then I remembered Daisy.

I don't know how I made my way back to Bessie alive. The water was hurling everything imaginable at me. The floating wreckage I had to dodge now contained big chunks of houses, small shacks, outhouses, carriages, and whole trees. With the rough water churning and racing, the pieces of debris collided, bumping and grating against each other, creaking and groaning.

Panic had set in. Men, women, children, and animals were all trying desperately to reach higher ground. People shouted, screamed, and cried. Dogs barked as they swam frantically back and forth through the water. A group of horses whinnied as they passed me, moving west. Cows bawled and lambs bleated as water filled the barns. Chickens squawked, roosting on anything that stuck above the water. And, above it all, the wind howled, sending chills up and down my spine. It sounded like the city was coming apart.

I was glad to finally reach Thirty-third Street. I was about to turn left when I heard someone shout at me above the wind, "Don't go! You can't go through there, it's too deep—there's a deep hole." I had to turn back and go down Thirty-second. It's only ten blocks from my house to Madame Matisse's, but I feared I would never get there. I was frantic to reach Daisy.

All along, I'd seen houses breaking apart and joining the floating drift. So you can imagine my relief when I reached Thirty-third and Avenue S and saw Madame Matisse's house still standing and all in one piece.

The first floor was flooded, so I had to look for another entrance. On the north side of the house, I spotted an old oak tree overhanging the second-floor. I tied Bessie as tightly as I could to the oak. Then, with the wind tearing at my clothes, I shinnied up the tree. Daisy must have spied me coming, for she ran to the French doors that open onto the balcony. But the wind was blowing against them and they would not open.

I gripped the balcony railing and worked my way around to the south door. My back muscles ached, and my knuckles turned white from holding on so tightly.

Daisy was waiting. She threw her arms around me. "Oh, J. T.," she said, "you poor thing! We must get you some dry things!" I told her there wasn't time. I explained that I had come to get them. The water was rising fast, and the current was growing stronger by the minute. We had to hurry if we were going to make it to my house before the storm reached hurricane force.

Daisy prepared to go, but her mother refused to budge. "Daisy, you may go if you wish, but I'm waiting for Cornelius," she announced, crossing her arms defiantly across her stomach. Her stomach was awfully big from the child she was expecting.

"Mrs. Larchmont," I said, standing at the south window, "you cannot wait any longer. Please come see." I pointed to the flooded streets below. "Look," I said. Reluctantly, she walked to the window.

Several families were wading in the streets, heading for higher ground. As we watched, a huge pile of floating rubbish struck a woman from behind. It knocked her little girl out of her arms and into the rushing waters. The child was carried swiftly downstream away from her mother.

Mrs. Larchmont screamed. "Do something!" she cried, digging her fingernails into my arm.

Down in the street, the woman swam like mad after her daughter. The water flowed faster than a grown man can run. Then the little girl was caught up in an eddy. Round and round she went. All that circling gave her mother the time she needed to catch up to her. Frantically, the mother managed to pluck the little girl out of the spiraling water.

"Oh!" said Mrs. Larchmont, sobbing and burying her face in her hands. "All right," she said, " I'll go. But you must take us to Larchmont Hall. I must see Cornelius."

"Okay," I told her in desperation. It was a lie. I knew we'd never make it all the way to Broadway. It'd be by the grace of God just to make it to Momsie's. But I had to get Mrs. Larchmont and Daisy out of there, and I couldn't tell her about Mr. Larchmont yet.

Madame Matisse would not go with us. *"Mon cheri, I saw rougher water than this when I crossed the Atlantic from France,"* she said. She was going to ride out the storm at home.

Madame Matisse led us down an inside stairwell with access to a first floor window not yet under water. I squeezed through first so I could bring the wagon around. Then I put Daisy and her mother in the wagon bed and covered them with blankets. The rain felt like hail when it struck my face.

We were facing death. To head east for Momsie's, we had to travel against a mighty current. I kept the wagon away from the middle of the road, where the water ran the fastest.

Wood, slate, and glass whizzed over our heads, threatening to cut them off. I had to go slowly because electric wires were down in the water. Blown about by the wind, the wires leapt wildly in the air, popping and snapping, frying snakes and zapping fish that swam too close.

That spooked Bessie, so, for the last six blocks, I got down from the wagon and led her by a rope. Once the current knocked me down and tried to carry me away. But, fortunately, as I floated past Bessie, I was able to grab her forelegs and hold on. I knew I must save myself if I were to save Daisy. I struggled to my feet and trudged on.

When we reached the corner of Avenue Q½ and Twenty-seventh, the wind shifted from north to east, and things got really bad. The wind was dead against us, blowing a gale. It got very dark. The water rose very quickly, lapping against Bessie's belly and hitting me in the chest. The wagon began to lift and float. Bessie refused to walk a step further. We were three blocks from safety. I knew if we didn't get a move on, we'd drown in minutes.

I thought fast. I tore off my rain slicker and threw it over Bessie's eyes. I walked beside her, yelling encouragement and assurances in her ear. Somehow I managed to get her moving again. We made it to the house.

Momsie had lowered a ladder to the street for us from the first-floor porch. I helped Daisy and Mrs. Larchmont up the rungs. The ladder shook as Mrs. Larchmont climbed it. She no longer demanded to be taken to Larchmont Hall.

I could hardly stand against the wind now. In the water, I spotted several long, sturdy planks rushing by our house and grabbed them. I built a ramp over the back steps for Bessie to walk up. We were just about inside the house when the wind tore the rain slicker from my hand, whisking it away.

I took one last look before going inside. Now that the wind had shifted, the storm was really letting loose. While that north wind had blown, it had kept back the Gulf waters. In those several hours, the water had piled up. Now, with the wind blowing out of the east, there was nothing to stop the Gulf waters from breaking loose and covering the city. I watched as the storm tide rolled up Twenty-fifth Street toward me. Huge waves slid over the surf of the tide and broke against second-floor windows.

From the looks of it, I knew the worst was yet to come.

3:30 P.M.

When I entered the house, I was surprised to find it full of neighbors—some I knew and some I didn't. A few wore bathing suits. One family had brought their milk cow into our house and another carried a box full of kittens. Many of them were homeless, their houses gone to pieces. Others had tried to reach the middle of the city, but found the streets blocked off by floating timber. They were forced to turn back and look for shelter. They picked our house because it was known as the strongest in the neighborhood.

Momsie welcomed everyone. She gave them blankets, buttered toast, and hot coffee. Mr. Plummer gave first aid to people gashed by flying slate. Mrs. Newton found some dry clothes for Daisy and even a maternity dress for her mother. Momsie took Mrs. Larchmont into her room to lie down for a spell. Samson passed out apples to the children.

Everyone was talking about the storm. "Even Broadway is flooded!" one woman reported. That meant only one thing. If the highest ground in the city was underwater, then all parts of Galveston were underwater. The waters of the bay and the waters of the Gulf must have met in the middle of the city and swallowed it. Only the roofs of houses, treetops, and telephone poles must have been poking above the sea, like toys in a kid's bathtub.

The wind was blowing furiously. If a door or a window were to blow open or shatter, the roof would lift off our house and the walls would cave in. We went around closing the green storm shutters on the outside of the windows and nailing boards across the inside. I nailed an oak table leaf inside the back door and an ironing board against the front one.

With the doors and windows shut tight and so many wet people inside, the house felt hot and sticky. It was very dark. Mr. Plummer oiled and lit three old kerosene lamps and set them around. They cast spooky patterns on the ceiling, but we were grateful for the light.

4:00 P.M.

We knew that something awful was happening. Never had there been such a terrible storm. I was nervous for my friends. How was Ippy? I wondered. And Willie and Al and Frank? And what about Crab Jack? He lives right on the bay shore.

Daisy and I peeked through a crack in a boarded-up window and looked out. What we saw scared us to death. The sea ran as high in the streets as it did in the Gulf. We watched as one by one the houses south of us washed off their foundations and slid into the sea. It looked as if we would be next.

Higher and higher the water climbed, engulfing our front steps. We could hear the salt water lapping against the sides of the house. My sturdy house felt like a shaky old boat at sea. I could feel it rocking, surrounded by water, with the water growing closer, ever closer. It was as black as night outside. The lightning crackled, and the thunder roared. With each terrific gust of wind, the house creaked and groaned, as if in grueling pain.

We started to think the water might come inside the house. We got busy moving things upstairs. The men rolled up the carpet in the sitting room and hauled it upstairs. Others started moving the foodstuffs. The women carefully gathered up Momsie's china, silver, and cut glass. I put Papa's sword in Mr. Plummer's room. I watched Momsie take Popeye's photo out of its frame and tuck it inside her blouse.

I thought, "What do I want to save?" Immediately, I knew—my diary. I dashed to my room and rummaged through my drawers until I found an old square of oil-cloth. Carefully, I wrapped both my diary and pen in the waterproof fabric. Then I yanked my brand new rain slicker off the wall peg and put it on. I tucked the package snugly in its watertight pocket, sealing the heavy flap. Confident that my treasure was safe, I rejoined the others.

Mrs. Larchmont's face was all blotched and red. She looked as if she'd been crying. Momsie must have told her about her husband's death. Nevertheless, she helped the other women fill pitchers of fresh water and carry them upstairs. Daisy put Bessie and the milk cow in one of the west bedrooms.

It was good to have something to do. It gave us less time to think.

We all knew what was coming. The terrible storm that had raged around us for the last several hours was closing in on us.

4:30 P.M.

To leave the house was to drown. The gray Gulf waves looked like they were hitting the sky. There were waves on top of waves, always breaking higher and higher. The noise from the storm was deafening. The heavy rain pounded bare wood on the roof—all the shingles had been ripped off by the wind. It sounded like a freight train crossing the ceiling. With no shingles to keep out the rain, it dripped into the house. Momsie set out pans in the upstairs bedrooms to catch the drops to try to keep the house dry.

But it was no use. The rainwater penetrated the plaster of the walls. Bubbles formed behind the wallpaper and popped like firecrackers. Chunks of plaster fell from the ceiling and from the walls. Every once in a while, a flying shingle slammed against the house like a cannonball, making us jump out of our skins. Trees uprooted by the rushing waters crashed against our house, scraping and banging.

5:00 P.M.

The wind was blowing furiously against the front door. The men took turns standing against it to keep it shut. Luckily, Samson remembered all those wooden cases of root beer Momsie had bought for the medical students. We hauled them out of the pantry and stacked them high in front of the door to brace it.

About sixty people were huddled inside our house. Every one of us was frightened out of our wits. People were praying and singing and weeping. Momsie played the piano to try to drown out the storm. Mr. Plummer sang "A Mighty Fortress Is Our God."

5:30 P.M.

Samson got his ax and chopped holes in the floor of the sitting room and downstairs hallway. It pained me to see him do that to Momsie's beautiful solid oak floor. But he said it might save us. He said the holes would let the water into the house and help anchor it to its foundation. I stuck a pencil down one of the holes to see how high the water was already under the house. The tip of the pencil came back wet.

We were moving some pieces of furniture upstairs when the water came in. It slid in a sheet under the front door. Fargo ran over and barked at the flowing water when he saw it creeping across the floor toward him. He tried to bite it back, but the water kept coming anyway. He ran and jumped in Daisy's lap. We were all surprised to find ourselves laughing at such a terrifying moment.

6:00 P.M.

It was amazing to see how fast that water rose. It rose as fast as water flows into a bathtub. You could watch the water climb higher and higher against the walls. Parents scooped up their children to put them up on the piano, the dining room table, the sofa.

But then the piano stool began floating, as did the side tables holding cups of coffee and plates of buttered toast. The water was rising too fast for us to stay on the first floor. We all hurried to the stairs.

6:15 P.M.

We huddled on the dark stairway, with only an oil lamp, listening to the terrible storm. We could hear the creaking of the front porch as it broke apart. I could picture the rail posts sailing into the air like straws. Upstairs, the window blinds were slamming. Each howl of the wind was followed by the crashing of houses. It was awful.

We expected the house to go any minute. It was shaking back and forth so badly.

The water began to creep up the stairs. We squeezed as high as possible at the very top.

6:30 P.M.

Suddenly the wind blew a tidal wave into our house. I promise—that water rose four feet in four seconds! The rush of water was so sudden and so powerful that it swept everyone off the bottom six steps, including me. We swam about in the dark. Then someone shone a lantern, and I was able to find the surface. I then heard Samson yelling, "Over here!" He tossed us some rope, and we pulled ourselves back to the stairs.

Everyone was screaming and pushing up the stairs to get away from the water. It was almost as if the water was chasing us. The children were crying. We herded everyone into the back west bedroom upstairs. We managed to cram everybody into what we thought was the safest room left in the house. Samson and I found some old boards in the attic and boarded up the windows in the other bedrooms. Then we shut those doors and joined the others.

You cannot imagine the sound of the wind. It was blowing out of the south, right at us. It wanted into our house so badly. It pounded on the windowpanes and rattled the shutters. We had to keep it out or we were done for.

7:00 P.M.

Everyone crowded into the upstairs bedroom, frightened to death. We heard a heavy thumping noise coming from downstairs. It sounded as if someone were striking the ceiling with a hammer. I went to investigate. I walked to the top of the stairwell and shone my lantern.

The dim light did not reveal the old familiar stairs and banister. Instead, the orange glow of the lantern landed as if on a floating mirror. I was looking at the sea. The water had risen inside our house to the top of the stairs. The heavy thumping we heard was the sound of furniture on the first floor bumping against the ceiling as the water level rose and fell.

Soon the water would be on the second floor of our house. Popeye would never have believed it.

We heard a tremendous explosion down the hall, followed by a crashing of blinds and a shattering of glass. One by one, the windows blew out of the other upstairs bedrooms. Our ears popped as the wind rushed in. Behind those closed doors, the wind was making spooky sounds. It sounded as if a thousand tiny devils were running around the rooms, shrieking and whistling to get out.

Once the wind had gotten in, we waited for the house to fall. The end was near. Some people knelt in prayer. Others sang hymns. People were weeping, wailing, clutching each other. Children clung to their mothers. I heard someone ask, "Which do you think will get us first—the wind or the water?"

But I knew it wouldn't be either one. There was yet a third, more urgent, danger. I had spied it from the south bedroom window when I was nailing up boards. At first, it had been too dark to see out the window. But then the clouds parted, letting the moon shine on the street below. Only there was no street anymore— only a raging sea, fifteen to twenty feet deep. It was a world of whirling chaos.

The size of the waves alone made my hair stand on end. I bet they were thirty feet high. But my blood ran cold when I saw what the huge waves were pushing ahead of them. It was an enormous wall of wreckage, at least three stories tall. In that ridge were houses, buggies, furniture, fences and, of course, thousands of dead bodies, and—what I feared most—gigantic segments of the streetcar track that used to run along the beach. Slowly the waves were shoving that pile of wood and steel north—right toward us.

No house, no matter how sturdily built, could stand up to such a battering ram. Our house was going to collapse. We were doomed to be swept under with it. Last night's dream—was it a premonition? "Island of Doom"—that's what Malhado means, what Cabeza de Vaca had called our island. Boy, was he right!

I needed a plan for escape. Instinct had to guide me.

Momsie helped get people ready to leave the house. She found a pair of sewing scissors and helped the women cut off their long hair so it wouldn't get tangled in the wreckage. Mrs. Larchmont agreed to it, but Mrs. Newton refused. Her red mane is her crowning glory, she said, and she refused to part with it.

Everybody in that hot, sweaty, cramped, and dark room expected each moment to be his last. But not I. I was convinced I would come out of this one alive. Into my mind popped a story I had heard of a man who was the sole survivor of a sinking ship. As the ship went down, the man crawled onto a wooden plank. He drifted on this raft five miles to shore. Instinct was telling me how we could survive. And I was listening.

As strongly as I could, I warned everyone there that the house was getting ready to collapse. I had to shout to be heard over the storm. "When the dangerous moment comes," I urged them, "jump out a window. Grab anything washing by and float on it."

Suddenly the house began to shift. People scrambled about, panic-stricken, looking for something to cling to, some place to hide. But it was useless. The only escape was to join the storm. We needed an exit. I managed to pry open three windows. Samson then used his ax to smash through the wooden storm shutters.

We paired up. Mrs. Newton tied a trunk strap around her baby and fastened it to her waist. Momsie put her arm around Mrs. Larchmont. I held Daisy's hand. Mr. Plummer was looking after Hank. Samson had Fargo in a sling around his neck and, with rope, tied himself to Hal. Then we lined people up beneath the windows and prepared them to jump. I did not know what to do about the kittens, Bessie, and the milk cow. Bessie had been a faithful old mule. I would never see her again.

And then it happened. The house began moving off its foundation. It felt like we were in a boat being lifted by a giant wave. I had been standing guard at the northwest window, watching for a piece of drift to float by that was sturdy enough for my group to climb onto. I knew that, any minute, the house would go.

The house began to tilt onto its side. Then, as if in answer to a prayer, an upended roof floated right up underneath our window. I climbed on first to see if it was stable before yelling, "Jump!" The night was so dark that I couldn't make out the figures who managed to join me before the roof cut loose and sailed off into the storm.

I looked back in time to see the surging waters whisk my house away. The waves began tearing it to pieces. Anyone left inside the house was trapped.

We were swept away into the Gulf.

I was frantic to know who had escaped from the house. "Momsie!" formed in my throat, but nothing came out. Then as lightning flashed brilliantly around me, I could see her huddled with Daisy and Mrs. Larchmont, who clung to Momsie. As lightning flashed again, Daisy made her way toward me across the up-turned roof. Off in a corner, Mr. Plummer shielded Hank between his legs. A few feet away, Samson sat with his arm around Hal while Fargo still hung in a sling around his neck. I scanned the area again and again. Everyone in our little group was accounted for but Mrs. Newton and the baby. Where were they? They were not anywhere on our "raft."

Panic-stricken, I looked into the water rushing by. In such total darkness, though, it was impossible to tell people from driftwood. I cupped my hands, calling out over the roar of the storm, "Over here! Over here!" but nobody ever answered. Mrs. Newton and the baby were nowhere to be found.

It didn't seem possible that I should live while a mother and a child should die. I was sick with grief. I had heard that drowning people grabbed onto things floating by, so I dangled my feet in the water. Driftwood bashed my shins and snakes swam by my legs. I couldn't stop thinking of sharks and devilfish, but I kept my legs in the water anyway. Finally, I gave up. No one else was out there. Our little group now numbered nine.

Yet the waves showed no mercy. We were soon pitched from the roof and forced to cling to smaller drift. The waves would shoot high in the air and tear away our drift. It was all we could do to hang on as we moved from one piece of wreckage to another. Between the waves, we would raise our bodies and shout to each other.

The rain beat and whipped and cut. On larger pieces of drift, we could brace ourselves in sitting positions with our backs to the wind, holding broken pieces of plank behind our heads to protect ourselves from flying slate and bricks. The plunging waves shoved boxes, logs, planks, and objects big and little we had to dodge. If there was one monster wave that night, there were ten thousand. The waves would wash us north and then back again south. I lost all sense of direction.

For a good while, our group managed to stay together. But then a giant house came bearing down upon us, riding a big wave. It sat on its side, about eight feet higher than the drift on which we were riding. It was sweeping everything beneath it that lay in its path. We had one choice—climb up onto it or die.

When the house came within reach, I leapt up and got a good grip on the highest part of it. I called to Daisy and Momsie to grab on, too. I thought perhaps we could push the house down into the water and scramble on. Together, the three of us were able to lower the upper side. We had to be careful that it didn't come crashing down on us as it rose and fell with the waves.

We had starting pulling people onto the roof, starting with Mrs. Larchmont, when, unexpectedly, a monster wave struck. We were totally unprepared. We watched in horror as the wave swept Samson, Hank, Hal, Mr. Plummer, and Fargo off their drift and into the black swirling water.

Hal screamed, "Save me, save me!" and then the sea swallowed him up. All five of them were simply gone. As we stared in shock, a second monster wave hit, and then another. Then the rest of us four were knocked into the water.

Up until then, I had not allowed myself any thoughts of despair—I was determined to survive. But then, with so many loved ones gone, I thought of how easy it would be just to turn loose and open my mouth to the water. I was distraught. I could not imagine life without wise old Samson and dependable Mr. Plummer. I grieved for those helpless little boys. And Fargo—my faithful dog, Fargo.

But then I realized if I'm alive, Daisy and Momsie and Mrs. Larchmont might be, too. I thought of Mrs. Larchmont's unborn baby. I found myself swimming like mad toward a plank floating by. I grabbed it, keeping my head above the water, looking wildly for the others. Miraculously, I spotted three figures bobbing and kicked my way toward them.

Momsie, Daisy, and Mrs. Larchmont wept to see me. Together we were able to latch onto an upturned porch and pull ourselves up. For two more hours, we rode the waves. Strange and terrible things floated past us— dead horses and cows, carriages. We even dodged a baby grand piano riding the crest of a wave, its ivory keys gleaming in the dim moonlight. We were exhausted from clinging to timber. My back felt like red-hot wires were wrapped around it. Sharp knives plunged into my spine. I coughed from all the salt water I'd swallowed. I'd never been so cold. But I knew it couldn't stay dark forever. It had to be close to morning.

Just when I thought I couldn't hold on a minute longer, the wind shifted, and, with it, the tide. We began to float back toward land. A full moon came out and the skies began to clear. The storm appeared to be ending.

I looked over at Daisy. Her eyes were riveted on her mother. Mrs. Larchmont was sprawled on her back, her head in Momsie's lap.

"Is she hurt?" I cried.

"No, J. T.," Momsie said softly. "She's going to have her baby."

"Here?" I gasped. "On the water?"

"Don't worry, J. T.," said Momsie, in that calming way she has. "It won't be here for some time."

The waves brought us back into the city—what was left of it. The porch on which we were floating came to rest atop an enormous wall of debris. We found ourselves outside the upper windows of the Ursuline Convent. After that long night of drifting, we had landed only six blocks from our house.

And there, reaching toward us through one of the windows, were two of the Catholic sisters. Somehow they managed to haul us in. When they saw that Mrs. Larchmont was in labor, they hustled her away. Less than an hour before, we had thought ourselves alone in the world, but to our amazement, the convent was filled with other refugees from the storm. There must have been close to a thousand of them. And the sisters hurried to tend to us all.

The sisters gave us dry clothes and steaming bowls of oatmeal. It was only then that we realized how tired we all were. Daisy, Momsie, and I found a corner in the hallway outside Mrs. Larchmont's room and collapsed on the floor, against one another. Daisy fell asleep in Momsie's arm. We hoped that the next sound we would hear would be the high-pitched cry of a healthy newborn baby.

5:00 A.M.

It wasn't a baby that woke me but a dog. "Ruff! Ruff!" The bark echoed through the enormous convent. I opened my eyes. I knew that bark. It was Fargo's! Then I heard the tippy-tappy of his toenails striking the floor. I looked up to see him bounding toward me with Hal smack on his heels. Fargo jumped on my chest, licked my face, and wiggled all over, his tail wagging. Hal hugged my neck hard. Tears flowed down both our faces.

I peered over Hal's shoulder, expecting to see Samson right behind him. I looked all around, but I did not see him.

"Where's Samson?" I asked Hal.

He looked at the ground. "He's gone!" he said, sobbing.

Samson—gone? Then Hal told me what happened after the monster wave knocked him, Samson, and Fargo into the water. For a time, he had remained roped to Samson while Fargo hung in the sling. The three of them bobbed around in the waves for a while. Then Samson saw a cedar chest washing by and grabbed it by its leather strap. He lifted Fargo and Hal inside the chest. For what seemed to Hal like hours, Samson swam alongside them, gripping the strap of that chest. Then a piece of wood struck Samson in the head, knocking him out. It was then that he disappeared. He must have drowned. Hal cried himself to sleep, clutching Fargo, floating about in their little boat of cedar. The next thing he knew, their cedar chest had bumped against the windows of the convent. They had beached on the same wall of debris we had.

Samson dead. A dull ache grew inside me. And what about Mr. Plummer and little Hank? Somehow, I still held out hope that I'd find Mrs. Newton and the baby and the rest of them—alive.

At daybreak, I promised myself I would begin my search.

A little before dawn

The night had been full of twists and turns. I didn't know what to expect from one moment to the next. First, the mother superior, Mother St. Agnes, came out into the hall to report that Mrs. Larchmont had given birth to a healthy baby boy. Hurrah! we shouted, hugging each other and jumping up and down. A few minutes later she returned, summoning us all to Mrs. Larchmont's bedside for a baptismal ceremony. Evidently, some of the babies born this night have died, and the sisters had to give them hasty baptisms.

The baby was named Cornelius Albert Larchmont III. His black hair sticks straight up and his skin is all purple and rubbery. Here's the best part: Mrs. Larchmont picked me to be his godfather. And Momsie is his godmother.

How completely upside-down this storm has turned our world. Yesterday, Mrs. Larchmont wouldn't even let me speak to her daughter over the telephone. Today, I'm practically a family member!

Continuing Sunday, September 9, 1900

I cannot believe we survived that terrible storm. We started off today's Sabbath by falling on our knees and giving thanks to the Lord God Almighty for letting us see daylight again. We are badly bruised and cut and our nerves are rattled; we have no home, no food, and only the clothes on our backs; but we are alive and well—and we have each other. We count ourselves among the fortunate. The man who was praying beside me has lost everything—including his wife and three little girls.

Early afternoon

I just got back from combing the island. An eerie peace has settled over the convent. You'd expect to hear some screaming and crying and carrying on from people who have experienced so much death and trouble. But quite the opposite is true. People pace the halls in silence, as if in a trance. No one speaks. It's creepy. The refugees have on such weird clothing, too—nuns' habits, flour sacks, mattress ticking. Almost everyone is barefoot.

I was among the few people willing to go out in the city. I guess the others are terrified of what they (or their children) might see. We have heard some pretty gruesome stories already. Over on Heard's Lane, about a hundred bodies were found tangled in the top branches of some salt cedars. The corpses were covered with double-fanged snakebites.

Black slime from the bay coats everything. It stinks like rotting fish. With every step you take, we heard, you sink into the muck onto a dead body. Dead bodies and wreckage are everywhere. The city is in ruins. Nevertheless, I went out.

I had trouble from the start. First off, I couldn't get my boots on. My feet had swelled from too many hours in the water. I had made up my mind to go in my stocking feet when a kindly sister saw my predicament and brought me a pair of man's boots as big as shovels.

It was a good thing she appeared when she did, because I couldn't have made the trip without those boots. I soon discovered that in order to get to my side of the island, I had to climb over a two-story wall of wreckage. Without those boots, the pointed shards of glass, jagged wood, and slate in that trash heap would have sliced my feet to ribbons.

Words cannot describe the view that awaited me at the top of that mountain. The city I love has been reduced to a pile of rubble. The Gulf side of the island has been swept bare, as if by a broom. All that's left of the houses are mounds of splinters.

A passage leading into my old neighborhood has been cut through the hill of wreckage, and I went through it. The sides of the passage are over thirty feet high. At first, I could not tell where I was. Almost no landmarks remain. Most buildings have been destroyed. Railroad tracks are twisted and broken, trees uprooted, telephone poles flattened, and wires ripped loose.

Once I spotted the Bath Avenue Public School, my old school, I knew I was three blocks from home. The school has been badly damaged. A wall has been ripped away from one of the classrooms, and I could see inside. The classroom hangs over the street at a forty-five degree angle, its desks still anchored to the floor in neat rows.

People were wandering the streets in a daze, looking for the bodies of their missing babies, grandmothers, husbands. "Have you seen my wife?" one man asked me. I asked around, but no one had seen Samson, Mr. Plummer, or the three Newtons.

I came to the corner of Twenty-fifth and Q½. Where just hours ago my house had stood was only scattered wreckage.

I struggled to get my bearings—I determined where the pretty Neville house had been, and Mr. and Mrs. Cline's and Dr. Young's houses. Where Murdoch's once stood is now only open sky. I looked far down the beach for the familiar silhouette of St. Mary's orphanage with its roof of crosses, but saw just a long white arc of empty sand. Everywhere I looked was wreckage. When I looked more closely at the piles, I could see cradles and chairs, striped dresses and straw hats—and arms and legs. I threw up.

People were picking through the ruins of their homes and I began to do the same, not knowing what I hoped to find but afraid of what I might. When I saw a bright shock of red hair, I knew instantly what it was. I lifted some boards and gazed down on the faces of Mrs. Newton and her baby, still tied to her mother's side.

There was a faint smile on Mrs. Newton's face. Her hair was not gorgeous anymore. It was matted and streaming in wild confusion about her shoulders. Her body had stiffened in the position in which she had drowned—arms overhead, trying to free her hair from the snarl of wood and wires that had dragged her underwater and taken her and the baby's lives.

I borrowed a shovel and dug a shallow grave in the mud, laying mother and child in it. I covered their faces with an old washboard I found nearby. I buried them as best I could, mounding the mud on top of the grave and, at its head, sticking three stray posts upright in the ground for a marker.

I looked out to sea. It was deadly calm.

Much later that night

We knew we couldn't stay at the convent much longer. Food and water were running low, yet people kept arriving. Momsie, Daisy, and I paced the floor, racking our brains to figure out where in a wrecked city we could take a bedridden mother, her new baby, a six-year-old boy, and an extremely short dog.

We were growing quite discouraged when, along about suppertime, we heard the tap-tap of somebody running. We turned to see Moses sprinting down the great hall of the convent toward us.

Tears streamed down his face. "You're alive!" he shouted, so loudly that others camped in the hall turned to stare. I could see his eyes scanning the place for Samson. I caught his eye and shook my head sadly. He looked to the ground.

Moses insisted on going right away into Mrs. Larchmont's room. He had to see her with his own eyes. "Mighty clouds of joy!" he cried when he saw the new baby. Moses leaned over the bed and scooped up Mrs. Larchmont. "I'm taking you home!" he announced, carrying her down the hall and settling her carefully in a wagon he borrowed from a friend living on a part of the island that wasn't hit as hard as Broadway. Gone was the fancy carriage with the coat of arms on the door. Larchmont Hall still stood, he said, but much was damaged.

Momsie wrapped up the baby and handed it to Mrs. Larchmont, who insisted that Momsie and the rest of us come with them to Larchmont Hall. We thanked Mother St. Agnes and the kind sisters, and then we, too, climbed into the wagon.

Slowly, we negotiated the narrow passageways cut through the debris and mud. We passed dead bodies everywhere. Relief workers were carting them off on stretchers. Most of the bodies were naked and bloated. Their faces were so mutilated by the storm you couldn't tell who they were. One poor man was stopping any stretchers carrying dead women and looking into their mouths. Apparently he was searching for his wife. He was hoping to identify her by her dental work.

Larchmont Hall looked pretty good from the outside. Some oak trees were down in the yard and some shingles were off the roof. It was the inside that was a wreck, Moses told us. The floodwaters had risen six feet on the first floor, covering it in salt water and scum.

We found the servants lined up on the front porch, waiting to receive us. They escorted our group through the grand reception hall and up the winding staircase. As we passed by the Gold Room, Daisy and I peeked inside. The pink silk wallpaper and heavy crimson drapery were streaked with water stains. I saw only flecks of gold and white paint on the French antique sofa and four matching chairs because they were coated in black slime the consistency of axle grease.

Daisy gasped when she saw the parlor that had been so grand. "Mama will simply go to pieces!" she whispered in my ear.

But Mrs. Larchmont glanced into the Gold Room and shrugged her shoulders. Moses asked her if she wanted to inspect the house for damage before she retired to her room.

She gave a low chuckle. "No, Moses, oddly enough, I don't," she said. "I don't seem to care about my 'pretties' much anymore. It seems so foolish to think about things like that after witnessing so much human suffering. I can't stop thinking about all those people out there, hungry, homeless, and hurting. I have so much to give while others have so little. I feel I must do something to help them."

She was so weak. Moses carried her upstairs and propped her up in bed. She ordered Flossie to search the house for some dry writing paper and a pen. Meanwhile, Momsie dragged a rocking chair over to the bed and rocked the baby.

Mrs. Larchmont called Moses to her bedside. "Is there any food in the house?" she asked him.

"No, ma'am," he said. "That salt water soaked every bit of it."

"How are we fixed for drinking water, then?" she asked.

"Only the tank on the roof is fresh," he replied. "The two cisterns in the cellar are full of mud and brackish water."

Mrs. Larchmont thought for a minute. "Moses, you take the wagon back to the convent. Tell Mother St. Agnes to send over anybody in need of food or shelter."

She turned to me next. "J. T., I need you to run another errand." She scribbled a hasty note and handed it to me. "There. Take the cart," she said, "and run on down to the Tremont Hotel. Ask for Police Chief Ketchum and show him this note." The baby started crying. He was hungry.

I did as I was told. Once Chief Ketchum learned that Larchmont Hall had been turned into a refugee center, he wasted no time getting us the food we needed. He accompanied me to Focke, Wilkens, & Lange Wholesale Grocery Co., where we loaded sacks of potatoes, flour, oatmeal, ten-gallon cans of lard, and canned salmon onto my cart. Before he went back to the Tremont, he handed me a loaded pistol.

"Keep a sharp eye out, sonny," he said. "These streets are mean tonight."

I soon saw what he meant. It was growing dark and the looters were coming out. On my way down the Strand, I noticed some stores with broken windows. I could see shadows of men going in and out of downtown buildings in a most suspicious manner. I nudged the horse to pull the cart faster.

I was relieved to find four soldiers standing guard on the next corner. They formed an odd little army. All were barefoot. One fellow had on his pajamas and

115

another carried a bugle. I reported to them what I had seen and hurried back to the hall.

Monday, September 10, 1900

Early afternoon

Refugees are trickling in to Larchmont Hall. So far, about forty have arrived. Mrs. Larchmont welcomes everyone, white or colored, and even their animals. One family brought their pet milk cow. Now we can have some fresh milk.

Moses and I had the grim task of collecting Mr. Larchmont's body from the steamy warehouse that has become the morgue. The bodies were lined up in rows. The stench and the flies were so thick that we had to hold our breath and cover our noses and mouths as we searched also for Samson, Hank, and Mr. Plummer. I found myself looking too for Willie, Frank, Al, Crab Jack, and anyone I had not seen or heard from since Saturday. But the only body I recognized was Madame Matisse's. I hope someone comes to claim that brave lady.

After a short service at Eaton Chapel, we buried Mr. Larchmont in the family vault at the Episcopal cemetery. Mrs. Larchmont and Daisy bore up well under the strain. Later, back at Larchmont Hall, I saw Mrs. Larchmont choke back a sob when she spotted Mr. Larchmont's favorite smoking pipe sitting on a rack on top of his desk in his study.

That evening

Hallelujah! Mr. Plummer and Hank are alive! They appeared on our doorstep today—with quite an adventure story to tell, too. Adrift all night in the storm, they finally washed up on the East Beach. They found nothing standing except for one wall of a brick storeroom. On this wall was a shelf. On this shelf sat one bottle of beer and a can of sardines. For the first time in his life, Mr. Plummer said, "Yes!" to a beer! He didn't say, but I suspect he split it with Hank. They are exhausted and rather beat up.

Momsie has not left Mr. Plummer's side. I always knew they liked each other, but not this much. Now Hal has a brother again.

I found Ippy just where I'd hoped—at Western Union, working his heart out. He and his family rode out the storm at Grand Union Depot. We plan to get together after he gets off work Wednesday. So many Western Union messengers were killed in the storm, he said, that he must work twelve or fourteen hours a day.

I toured the hospitals, but still could not find any of the missing ones. When I was out in the streets, I kept running into people I knew. I could tell from their faces whether their loved ones were missing. Yet all I could say was, "I'm so sorry..." and go on my way, stepping around the dead to get home.

I hurried back to Larchmont Hall. I was glad to hear the heavy front door as it shut behind me.

I am safe. For a few hours, I can let myself forget the horror that lies outside these thick walls.

Tuesday, September 11, 1900

A boat from Houston arrived today, and Mr. Newton was on it. Hank and Hal were wild to see him. Mr. Newton had heard about his wife's and baby's deaths. I took him to their grave. Later, when I returned, I saw that he had set up a little board marked with their names on top of the grave until he could arrange for their proper burial in St. Louis.

Every minute, it seems, a fire wagon clatters by, loaded with corpses. They've given up burying them because the ground's too soggy. With this much heat— the temperature was eighty-eight degrees yesterday— the risk of disease is high. So now they're loading the bodies on barges and dumping them out in the Gulf. They're making the Negroes do the gruesome work and bribing them with whiskey. Some soldiers with bayonets tried to force Moses onto a barge, but Chief Ketchum intervened on his behalf.

"Leave him be, boys," said the police chief. "He's needed over at the refugee center."

Moses and I take turns guarding the water tank. Mrs. Larchmont says it's only for drinking, but I saw some people using it to wash their tubs of muddy clothes! If we're not careful, we'll run out before the tank cars bring in water later this week.

Mr. Plummer is helping to rebuild the four bridges leading to the mainland. He works on the night shift. Momsie cries when he leaves.

With each passing day, I lose hope of ever seeing Samson, Crab Jack, and the three orphans alive again.

Somebody said another storm is coming. Oh, Lord, no—

Wednesday, September 12, 1900

Midmorning

My stomach is churning. Samson's name was listed among the dead in this morning's newspaper. His body was dumped in the Gulf, no prayers, no burial, no nothing. Just one more body to dispose of. How will we ever do without him?

More bad news. A rescuer walking down the beach came across the corpse of a toddler. He tried lifting it but found the child was attached to a clothesline buried in the sand. He pulled on the clothesline. It sprung from the sand, revealing yet another child's body. He continued to pull and the line continued. The man found eight children buried on the beach, tied by a length of clothesline to a Catholic sister. They were all identified as having lived at St. Mary's Orphan Asylum.

We think everyone from the orphanage is dead—all ninety-three children and ten sisters. No trace of the buildings is left but a few scattered bricks. Mrs. Longino said the whole West Beach is strewn with bodies of little orphan children.

We're running low on water. I feel bad about leaving Moses to guard the cistern alone today. He's so sad over Samson. But I just have to connect with Ippy. He and I are desperate to find out what happened to Crab Jack. Mrs. Larchmont was kind enough to lend us the horse cart.

Afternoon

Bad things do come in threes. Ippy and I searched Crab Jack's lot, but could find no trace of his house. It was just wiped off the map. We were heading back to town when we heard, "Pretty Polly! Pretty Polly!" coming from the mudflats.

We found what was left of our boat, *Sailor Moon*, floating in the marsh. Perched on the bow was Lucky, Crab Jack's faithful parrot.

"Pieces of eight! Pieces of eight!" she squawked, flying over to rest on my shoulder. If only she really could talk. Then she could tell us what happened to Crab Jack. He was gone, that was obvious. I am going to miss him badly. But in death, he had reunited with his wife and his kids, and that comforted me somewhat.

Ippy and I will share Lucky. This week she's mine. Won't Hank and Hal get a kick out of a talking bird!

Thursday, September 13, 1900

Finally, some good news—

Willie, Al, and Frank aren't dead! On Sunday, some sailors on a ship spotted the three of them floating on a tree out in the Gulf. They took them to Fort Crockett. The waves had swept the orphanage into the sea, crushing or washing away every sister and orphan but the three of them.

Frank and Al have to stay in the hospital a while longer. Frank's skull is fractured, but Al's in even worse shape. He's talking out of his head. He keeps crying, "Save Maggie, save Maggie!" The nurses can't settle him down. Poor Al. Maggie is—or was—his little sister. He must have watched her die. Willie's over at his cousin's house. I need to get over there first thing. Willie's brother, Joe, is dead, I hear.

Dumping the bodies at sea didn't work. They're floating up on the beach by the wagonful. It's gruesome.

Friday, September 14, 1900

It looks as if the city's on fire. But it's not. As a last resort, Galveston is burning our dead. Twelve huge bonfires are blazing all over the city. Scorched hair and flesh smells sickeningly like burned sugar. It makes me want to throw up. It's about a hundred degrees today. There's nowhere to escape the heat—I'm not about to cool off with a swim. I wonder if I'll ever go in the sea again.

I saw Willie today. He has a big bandage wrapped around his left hand. He must still be in shock because he just sits around and doesn't say much.

I found out later how Joe, Willie's brother, died when the orphanage went under. Joe had been holding Willie's hand when the building went. Something fell down on Willie's hand, causing him to let go of Joe. Willie never saw his brother after that.

Willie, Al, and Frank may be sent to St. Joseph's in Houston. I don't want them to go. We must build a new orphanage to replace St. Mary's. But how ever will we do it?

Monday, September 17, 1900

Early this morning I took Mr. Plummer some fresh clothes and food. He's sleeping in a Pullman car next to the bridges where he lays track. He was glad to see me. "Let's walk out to Bay Bridge," he said. He wanted to show me his work. Before we had gone a mile, we saw men running ahead of us and hiding in the grass. Mr. Plummer thought they might be the men Chief Ketchum had warned him about—hoodlums who'd been stealing jewelry off bodies floating in the bay.

Tuesday, September 18, 1900

Finally they've brought us some water from the mainland. Otherwise, I don't know how we would have managed. One hundred people are camping at Larchmont Hall, and one hundred people use a lot of water.

Yesterday was a big day in the city's history. We all went down to the wharf to welcome the president of the Red Cross, Clara Barton. She's come to help us. Things will get better soon now that she's arrived. When Mrs. Barton speaks, the world listens. Things are already improving. The army has sent food, clothing, and tents from the Spanish-American War. Many of our refugees are leaving to pitch tents on their own property.

Hal is having nightmares. The smell of burning death hangs over the island. We live in it. We breathe it. We eat it. We drink it, day after day.

Chief Ketchum made a trip out to Larchmont Hall. He told Mr. Plummer that his men shot several looters yesterday. Their pockets were filled with rings and earrings, some still on fingers and ears that were cut from the corpses they'd robbed. The police had also confiscated other valuables the looters had taken from the wreckage. Chief Ketchum had brought one of those valuables to me.

"J. T.," he said, "do you recognize this?" He held up a sword. "One of the looters was carrying it."

"Oh, yes!" I cried. "That was Papa's, from the Spanish-American War!" He handed me the sword. I think I must have embarrassed him by thanking him too much. His face turned beet red and, with a quick tip of his hat, he bolted from the house and into the street.

Once we recover from this storm, I will never ever eat another bite of canned salmon.

Outsiders can never fathom what has happened here. They simply can't—no matter how much I write.

Wednesday, September 19, 1900

The Newtons left this morning by boat. Many people are leaving the island, some of them for good. There is even talk of abandoning the island and starting a new town on the mainland.

But the Larchmonts, Mr. Plummer, Momsie, and I are digging in our heels and staying. We are managing our grief with hard work. The rail bridge should be finished by Friday next. Then we'll be reconnected to the mainland and Mr. Plummer can come home. Home—

good as Mrs. Larchmont has been to us, Momsie and I are eager to return to a home of our own.

Thursday, September 20, 1900

Thanks to Clara Barton, help is pouring in. The story of the great Galveston hurricane has been on the front page of newspapers from Miami to London. We've received a ton of contributions. Some of the goods these charities send are funny. One person donated a case of fancy women's shoes, but all 144 of them were for the left foot. The shoes were samples from the kit of a traveling shoe salesman.

Work crews are clearing the lots and putting up new houses—including ours, on our old lot. Can anything smell as wonderful as fresh lumber? It fills our noses and drives away the stench of death. Yet the dead still lie under nearly every fallen house. We'll probably never know how many actually died in this great storm. Some people say Galveston has lost eight thousand people.

Monday, October 8, 1900

Today we moved into our new house. Mr. Plummer carried Momsie over the threshold. They got married

Saturday! How wonderful to be under our own roof again. With Momsie remarried, she won't need to take in roomers anymore! I have a big bedroom upstairs again. Our fireplace isn't finished though. Until then, Papa's sword will have to hang over the front doorway.

The Red Cross has pretty much cleaned up the island. Cotton is flowing into the port, and business is starting to return to normal. School starts October 22. Ugh.

The bonfires are still burning. Will they ever stop?

Ippy was riding his delivery bike yesterday when all of a sudden it fell apart. It had rusted from the inside out. All that salt water from the storm corroded it.

I am so thrilled! Willie, Al, and Frank are going to stay in Galveston. Mrs. Larchmont and her Wednesday Club are raising money to build a new St. Mary's Orphan Asylum. Mrs. Larchmont is organizing a fundraising bazaar and auction. She's even written to Queen Victoria of Great Britain and asked for her endorsement! Then she contacted all her rich New York friends. I've never seen the likes of their donations: costly furs, tiger rugs, opera cloaks, ladies' hats, silverware, watches, jewels, bicycles, a grand piano, and even an automobile.

The bazaar will be held at the end of this month at the Waldorf-Astoria Hotel in New York City. Our boat leaves on the 26th. Mrs. Larchmont is paying our way. She says she couldn't bear to go without us. Momsie is in charge of the refreshments. Daisy and I will perform the balcony scene from *Romeo and Juliet*. Mr. Plummer will introduce Mark Twain, who is scheduled to speak.

Friday, October 12, 1900

Tonight Daisy and I walked along the beach. The breeze blowing off the Gulf was chilly, so I draped my jacket across her shoulders. In the distance, we could see a campfire flickering. It gave off a cheery glow.

The two of us stood at the water's edge, holding hands. We took off our shoes and wiggled our toes in the cold, wet sand. The water rushed, foaming, over our feet and then the sea sucked it back again. I can't tell you how long we stood there, just Daisy and me, loving the ebb and flow of the tide, listening to the soft "sshhhh" of the waves and letting the salt air ruffle our hair. The sea was gentle tonight, almost hypnotizing.

The sea wants us to trust her again. But we have seen what she can do. She can swallow a man whole. In her rage, she rose up, took our loved ones, and destroyed our homes.

Now the sea is a drowsy giant, sleeping off her murderous rampage. But as poor Crab Jack well knew, she is no gentle thing.

As Daisy and I stood there on the beach, I clenched my fist and shook it at the sea. No, I can never trust her again. Like the island paradise we knew, that trust is gone forever.

Life in Galveston, Texas

1900

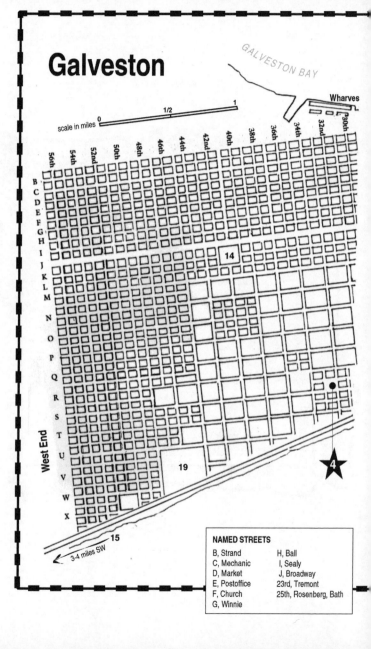

Galveston

GALVESTON BAY

Wharves

scale in miles 0   1/2   1

56th 54th 52nd 50th 48th 46th 44th 42nd 40th 38th 36th 34th 32nd 30th

B
C
D
E
F
G
H
I
J
K
L
M
N
O
P
Q
R
S
T
U
V
W
X

West End

14

19

15

3-4 miles SW

4

NAMED STREETS

B, Strand
C, Mechanic
D, Market
E, Postoffice
F, Church
G, Winnie

H, Ball
I, Sealy
J, Broadway
23rd, Tremont
25th, Rosenberg, Bath

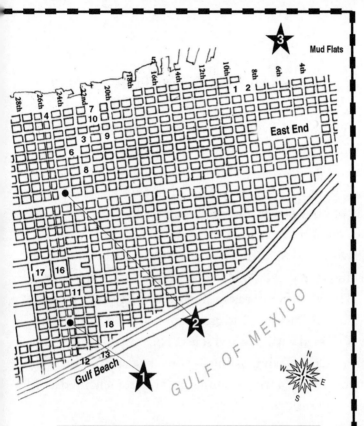

HISTORICAL SITES

1. University of Texas Medical Department ("Ole Red")
2. Sealy Hospital
3. Levy Building (U.S. Weather Bureau)
4. Grand Union Depot (Santa Fe Railroad)
5. Pier 16
6. Tremont Hotel
7. temporary morgue (Mensing Bros. and Co. cotton warehouse)
8. Eaton Chapel
9. Grand Opera House
10. Ritter's Cafe
11. Bath Avenue Public School
12. Murdoch's Bath House and Pier (with Bon Ton Restaurant)
13. the Midway

14. Episcopal Cemetery
15. St. Mary's Orphan Asylum
16. Ursuline Convent
17. Garten Verein (Garden Club)
18. skating rink
19. Fort Crockett

FICTIONAL SITES

⭐ 1 J.T. King's house
⭐ 2 Larchmont Hall
⭐ 3 Crab Jack's house
⭐ 4 Madame Matisse's house

Galveston and the Great Storm of 1900

By the year 1900, Galveston was the most sophisticated city in Texas. It boasted the most important port, the best newspapers and theater, and the greatest variety of sports. It was the first to have electricity and telephones. Twenty-six millionaires lived in mansions designed by such world-class architects as Nicholas J. Clayton and Stanford White. Galveston was elegant; it had style. It was called "the New York City of the Gulf."

The island city was indeed a "seat of good living." Besides its business and entertainment opportunities, it was blessed with rare and sensual beauty. Pink, fragrant oleanders, waving palms, sandy beaches, cool Gulf breezes, and warm, shimmering water enchanted visitors and residents alike.

Yet there were problems in paradise. "You have to tie yourself in bed at night," a visitor once complained, "to keep the cockroaches and other insects from carrying you off bodily. . . . If you attempted to sleep without a bar [mosquito net] . . . , there would be nothing but the bones of a person left in the morning." Epidemics of yellow fever plagued the city for much of the nineteenth century, often wiping out whole families. And then, of course, there were the hurricanes.

Galveston was beautiful yet fragile. It had placed itself in harm's way. Perched on the edge of land and sea, the seaport city lived always in the shadow of possible destruction by tropical storm. Galveston Island was not much more than a sand bar, really, sitting only nine feet above sea level at its highest point.

By the turn of the century, Galveston had experienced so many hurricanes that it had acquired a deadly reputation. Investors from other parts of the country began to shy away from investing more money in Galveston businesses that might one day be washed away.

Residents, however, were unconcerned. They had grown accustomed to their weird weather patterns. Storms generally brought wind and rain and a day off from work. As a result, Galvestonians did little to protect themselves from future storms. After Indianola was destroyed by hurricane in 1886, there was some talk of building a seawall, but interest faded, and nothing was ever done.

And then it was too late. On Saturday, September 8, 1900, a fierce hurricane pounded the island city of Galveston. It has been called the most devastating storm in the history of the United States. Galveston was reduced to a pile of rubble. Somewhere between six thousand and eight thousand people were killed.

We shall never know exactly how many died in the Great Galveston Storm of 1900. Bodies too numerous to identify littered the island. Emergency workers disposed of them in huge bonfires that burned from September to November. No one could guess how many more dead rested at the bottom of the sea. For several years, many people would not eat fish, shrimp, or crabs—anything that had come from that sea. An untold number of survivors sold their property, left the island, and resettled on the mainland.

Those who did not leave the city threw their energies into rebuilding it. Eleven days after the storm, a bridge connecting Galveston to the mainland was completed. Soon rail service resumed, and cotton once again began to flow into the harbor.

City planners then turned their attention to making Galveston safe for future generations. A team of engineers suggested a two-phased solution: building a seventeen-foot-high barrier along the Gulf side for three miles and raising the grade of the city behind the wall. Voters approved $2 million for the project.

More than thirteen thousand carloads of crushed granite, sand, cement, pilings, and steel went into the seawall, which was completed July 30, 1904. Then the second phase of the project was begun. For the next six years, more than twenty-one hundred buildings were jacked up so that the land beneath them could be filled in with sand. Everything had to be lifted up—streets, railroad tracks, water pipes, and fire hydrants, even trees and bushes. The largest building to be raised was St. Patrick's Church, weighing in at a full three thousand tons! At some places, the city was elevated seventeen feet.

In 1915, a more powerful hurricane than the 1900 killer storm hit Galveston. The seawall held. Citizens were cheered. Estimates vary as to how many people died, ranging from 4 or fewer to as many as 275. Over the ensuing years, improvements continued to be made to the seawall.

Today, visitors are still drawn to this tiny jewel set on the edge of the continent. It is a getaway spot, offering simple pleasures for everyone, young and old. Children toss breadcrumbs to seagulls hovering overhead. Families hold hands and wade into the gentle surf. Sunbathers lie on the hard-packed sand, listen to radios, and soak up some sun. Both visitors and old-timers fish from piers. Surfers ride the waves and sailboats bob in the harbor. Food tastes better here, eaten outside in the salty gulf breeze.

A weekend at Galveston acts like a tonic. After a few hours, worries begin to fade, homework is forgotten, and the workweek becomes a thing of the past. Although Galveston has never returned to its former glory, it has never lost its enduring charm.

Galveston Wharf Scene, Stockfleth, 1885, oil on canvas; The Rosenberg Library

It was the port that made Galveston strong. Immigrants poured in from Europe. Cotton was shipped out and cargo delivered.

The Rosenberg Library

Galvestonians in 1900 loved a parade. At one end of the route, orators waited to make patriotic speeches that filled all hearts with the glory of the occasion.

Library of Congress

Normally, the Gulf of Mexico is as warm and as gentle as a bathtub.

At Murdoch's Pier and Bath House, you could rent a bathing suit, fish off the pier, or eat ice cream at the Bon Ton.

By 1900, Galveston had replaced its mule-drawn streetcars with electric ones. One streetcar line ran along the Gulf beach, right over the water.

The Rosenberg Library

Galveston was covered by fifteen to twenty feet of water during the Great Storm of 1900. Some people were rescued in boats.

143

The Rosenberg Library

This photograph, taken between 1892 and 1896, features orphans in the care of the Sisters of Charity of the Incarnate Word. These Catholic sisters operated St. Mary's Orphan Asylum, three miles west of Galveston on the beach. All ten sisters and ninety of the orphans were killed in the Great Storm of 1900.

Next page: On the afternoon of September 8, 1900, the waters of the Gulf filled the first floor of St. Mary's Orphan Asylum on Galveston's West Beach. To calm the children, the sisters had them sing "Queen of the Waves," an old French hymn. It was traditionally sung during storms by fishermen seeking the protection of Mary, mother of Jesus—Queen of the Waves.

Queen of the Waves

The French hymn sung by the Sisters as they prayed for Our Lady's protection

1. Queen of the Waves, look forth a — cross the o — cean
2. But fear we not, tho' storm clouds round us gather,
3. Help, then sweet Queen, in our ex — ceed — ing danger,
4. Up to thy shrine we look and see the glimmer
5. Then joy — ful hearts shall kneel a — round thine altar

1. From north to south, from east to storm — y west,
2. Thou art our Moth — er and thy lit — tle Child
3. By thy seven griefs, in pi — ty La — dy save;
4. Thy vo — tive lamp sheds down on us a — far;
5. And grate — ful psalms re — ech — o down the nave;

1. See how the wa — ters with tu — mul — tuous mo — tion
2. Is the All Mer — ci — ful, our lov — ing Brother
3. Think of the Babe that slept with — in the man — ger
4. Light of our eyes, oh let it ne'er grow dim — mer,
5. Nev — er our faith in thy sweet power can fal — ter,

1. Rise up and foam with — out a pause or rest.
2. God of the sea and of the tem — pest wild.
3. And help us now, dear La — dy of the Wave.
4. Till in the sky we hail the morn — ing star.
5. Moth -er of God, our La — dy of the Wave.

The Rosenberg Library

Bath Avenue School can be seen in the foreground. A classroom hangs at a forty-five degree angle, its rows of desks still anchored firmly in place.

Life went on after the storm. This woman made her way through a clearing in the wreckage, possibly to wash clothes.

© Third Eye

About Lisa Waller Rogers

Lisa Waller Rogers remembers the day in 1970 when Hurricane Celia blew through Corpus Christi.

"It was a Saturday in August and I was fifteen years old. I lived in a two-story house just three blocks from the Gulf of Mexico. I had spent the morning packing because I was leaving for camp the next day. Everybody knew there was a hurricane out in the Gulf, but we weren't worried. It was no big deal. It had been stalled offshore for several days and didn't seem to be doing much. Anyway, we were used to storms hitting Corpus, and this was supposed to be a mild one.

"Boy, were we wrong! We were totally unprepared when, out of nowhere, that storm hit. It was about noon. By then it was too late to leave town, which is what my family had done in the last two hurricanes.

"That wind really came up fast. It picked up pebbles from our flat roof and hurled them at our windows. Dad got really worried that the glass would shatter. He ran around taping big Xs on the windows. He made my sisters and me sit on the stairwell, where there were no windows and it was safer. Our roof always leaked when it rained, so Mom ran upstairs and downstairs putting out pots and pans to catch the drips.

"You can't imagine the sound of that wind. It howled and beat on the house. Dad kept trying to get Mom to go sit on the stairs where she'd be safe, but she wouldn't get up. She was typing at the kitchen table, right in front of a large bank of windows. She said she had to finish transcribing some notes she'd taken at her law wives' meeting.

"But she got right up when she saw the water slipping in under the door. She grabbed towels and handed them around. We went around the house stuffing towels in windowsills and in the cracks below the doors. Mom got a broom and tried to sweep the water up. She wanted to save the carpet and furniture from flooding. Daddy got really mad at her because she was back in front of the windows again. He finally persuaded her to drop the broom and move to the stairs.

"Daddy was really nervous. I don't know where he got the cigarettes, but he smoked a lot of them during that storm. He hadn't smoked in six months, you see, so we were suspicious where the cigarettes had come from. Mom hated for him to smoke.

"Our two dogs, Anthony and Lady, were in the garage. The people in my family were huddled together on the stairs when my eleven-year-old sister, Laura, cried out, "I've gotta get my bird!" She had just remembered that she had left her yellow parakeet, Angel, in her upstairs bedroom. Daddy gave her permission to go up and get it.

"Laura had barely returned with her birdcage when we heard a terrific crash. It had come from Laura's bedroom. It sounded like a speeding train. We went up to see what had happened. We tried with all our might to push the door open, but it wouldn't budge.

"There was a little vent at the bottom of the door you could see through. I lay down on the hall floor and looked up through it. What I saw was unbelievable. The ceiling had a big hole in it, and I could see the sky. The wind had broken into Laura's room! It was acting like a miniature tornado. The wind was picking up things—stuffed animals, dolls, pillows, shoes, you name it—and whipping them around the room like a spinning top. It was a blur of color. It was probably raining in there, too, but mostly I remember the wind. It possessed that room.

"Finally the eye of the hurricane passed over, and we could go check on my sisters' room. Mom wanted us to try to save what we could before the second half of the storm came through and brought more rain. I remember her telling us to grab the valuables. I remember teasing Laura for grabbing 'Teddy' and 'Bunny,' her two favorite stuffed animals. I couldn't figure out how they could be considered 'valuables.'

"During the eye, we had a little more time before the storm started again. Mom was against it, but Daddy took us out into the front yard anyway. Everything was deadly calm. The wind and the rain had stopped completely. The light in the sky was a sickly yellowish green. The air was so stiflingly humid and hot that I found myself gasping for breath. It was creepy out there, so silent and so still.

"Our street was a mess. The fence between our house and our neighbors, the Sachniks, was down. We could see into their driveway. The windows in their green Rambler station wagon were all smashed up from a swing hanging in a nearby tree.

"The Tompkins, our neighbors on the other side, had a playhouse in their backyard. A tornado had picked it up and turned it upside down. Part of the playhouse was charred. It had been struck by lightning and had caught fire.

"In our front yard, one of our tall palm trees had snapped in half, like it was as flimsy as a toothpick.

"The next day, I went on to camp. Mom, Dad, and my sisters tried to stay in our house, but it was impossible. The electricity was out, and there was no air conditioning. It was beastly hot. Our house windows were nailed shut, so they couldn't crank them open for air. My sisters tried to sleep on the balcony, but the mosquitoes got to them. Daddy went nuts without his TV. He tried sitting in a lawn chair on the driveway listening to his battery-operated radio. Some friends came by and asked my family to move in with them for the week. They had air conditioning. My family wasted no time saying yes.

"Everybody missed the telephones. People had to get out in their cars to check on friends. It was dangerous because live power lines were down in the streets.

Mom got a flat tire from driving over some broken glass.

"Without electricity, it was impossible to keep food cold. A butcher drove through our neighborhood giving away meat from his storage vault because it had no refrigeration and the meat would spoil. Mom took the girls to a hamburger shop, where they were served warm limeade. There was no ice."

Hurricane Celia was a powerful storm, the costliest in the history of Texas. It had winds up to 161 miles an hour and gusts to 180 miles an hour. It did not, however, produce the torrential rains and flooding that brought such a terrific loss of life to Galveston in the Great Storm of 1900.

When Lisa Waller Rogers writes a history book, she wants it to be accurate as well as entertaining. She spends months in libraries gathering information young readers will find interesting. She reads old diaries, letters, newspaper articles, and journal entries written by real people who lived long ago. She discovers what they ate, read, wore, and did for fun. "Histories should capture the flavor of the times, not just the facts," she is fond of saying.

Ms. Rogers's first history, *A Texas Sampler: Historical Recollections,* was a finalist for the Texas Institute of Letters Best Book for Children/Young People Award. Her second book, *Angel of the Alamo,* received wide acclaim for its beautiful illustrations and Ms. Rogers's "obvious gift for storytelling," wrote Judith Rigler in the *San Antonio Express-News* (June 4, 2000). Book 1 in the Lone Star Journal series, *Get Along, Little Dogies: The Chisholm Trail Diary of Hallie Lou Wells,* debuted in spring 2001. Dr. Richard Sale, Professor Emeritus of English at the University of North Texas, considers this book "the ultimate Wild West adventure, complete with cowboys and Indians, hissing rattlesnakes, wolf packs howling at the moon, and a riproaring gunfight in a rowdy saloon." (*Texas Books in Review,* Spring 2001).

Ms. Waller Rogers is a sixth-generation Texan. She lives in Austin with her husband, Tom, their daughter, Katie, and four dachshunds: Fargo, Emma, Cookie, and Sammy Tomato.